ALSO BY DIMITRY ELIAS LÉGER

God Loves Haiti

DEATH
OF THE
SOCCER
GOD

DEATH OF THE SOCCER GOD

A Novel

DIMITRY ELIAS LÉGER

MCD FARRAR, STRAUS AND GIROUX
NEW YORK

MCD
Farrar, Straus and Giroux
120 Broadway, New York 10271

EU Representative: Macmillan Publishers Ireland Ltd, 1st Floor, The Liffey Trust Centre, 117–126 Sheriff Street Upper, Dublin 1, D01 YC43

Printed in the United States of America
First edition, 2026

Library of Congress Control Number: 2026003902
ISBN: 978-0-374-61988-6

10 9 8 7 6 5 4 3 2 1

Pour mes enfants, Sidney et Nina

And for my father, Jean Elias Léger, rest in peace

I'm a lucky man. I carry the world within me. You see, Salim, in this world beggars are the only people who can be choosers. Everyone else has his side chosen for him. I can choose. The world is a rich place. It all depends on what you choose in it.

—V. S. NAIPAUL, *A BEND IN THE RIVER*

Death of the Soccer God is a work of fiction inspired by actual events. While some characters are loosely based on real people, their characterizations, dialogue, and actions are products of the author's imagination. All references to actual individuals, entities, and events are made fictitiously.

CONTENTS

PART I: THE PRINCE OF PORT-AU-PRINCE

1. HAPPY DEATH DAY **3**

2. LES CHEVALIER OF THE CARIBBEAN **14**

3. HAITIAN FOOTBALL SONG **23**

4. NAZI LOVE **32**

5. JAZZ DES JEUNES **47**

6. AIMÉ OU AIMÉ **59**

7. CITÉ SOLEIL KISSES **66**

8. HARLEM BLUES **73**

PART II: GLORIOSO, MINEIRÃO

9. JOGO BONITO IN CENTRAL PARK **91**

10. ONE–NIL **103**

11. CIRANDAR **111**

12. O NOSSO AMOR **126**

13. TWO–NIL **131**

14. ORFEU NEGRO **137**

PART III: ALL-AMERICANA

15. CORCOVADO **145**

16. DREAMVILLE **153**

17. SKETCHES OF SPAIN **167**

18. PORT-AU-PRINCE ON LINE ONE **172**

19. HOMEGOING **174**

20. PRISON BREAK **190**

21. THE AMERICAN **194**

22. EXECUTION **201**

EPILOGUE **213**

ACKNOWLEDGMENTS **221**

PART I

THE PRINCE OF PORT-AU-PRINCE

So I replied to her: I cannot remember
That I ever strayed away from you,
Nor does my conscience bite me in that account.

And if you cannot recall any of that,
She answered smiling, now bring to your mind
How you have the water of Lethe today;

And if, as they say, there is no smoke without fire,
That forgetfulness of yours demonstrates clearly
A fault in your will—your attention was elsewhere

—DANTE, *THE DIVINE COMEDY*, PURGATORIO XXXIII

1

HAPPY DEATH DAY

Many years later, when Gilbert Chevalier faced a firing squad under a burning midday sun in the yard of Fort Dimanche, the worst place to be in Haiti, the volatile love of his life, and the captain shouted ready!, then aim!, to his ear, a long, pregnant pause preceded the final command, so Gilbert began begging God for mercy, while also begging the soldiers for a ceasefire, for the captain to take his time stretching the final order, delaying the coming mortal blows for as long as possible, because there were many guns aimed at him, the pain their bullets promised was going to be savage, and careless as he had been with the feelings of others his entire young life, Gilbert was not good with pain, and not at all ready to die, here, today, for no just reason he could think of, but the silence greeting his begging was loud and immense and not shrinking, and obviously wouldn't last forever, a terrifying concession by a reflexively optimistic man during this most awful moment of his life, the bitter end, so close, so unexpected, and so, so unwanted. His executioner exhaled, and the next breath would command fire, and breathe it out like a dragon, there would be explosions, dozens, fired bullets, torrents of them, and they would pierce his body and burn his entrails, enter through his eye sockets and shatter his brain, yes they would, they will, and the realization turned Gilbert's spine into soup, and then molten rage, making him hiss, seethe, eyes watering and widening in horror of the pending verdict of the glistening barrels of machine guns.

Machine guns! Fucking Haitians. They can't get most things right in life, but they're going to execute me. A mere football player. With machine guns! They're going to waste their ammunition on me, with ten men shooting at close range. Me! What's wrong with these people? Our planet? The universe! What the fuck?! Why is Haiti doing this to me? I never hurt anybody! Or broke a law other than the lightweight numbers of the Ten Commandments. So, what the fuck, God? Jesus! Please talk to Your father and get me out of this mess. What did I do in my life that was so wrong to deserve this fate? Talk to me, Lord. *Un peu de pitié quand même. Je mérite mieux.* Whisper the secrets of Your mercy, and my folly, in my ears. Surely You can do me this last favor, quickly, considering my predicament. You can move faster than speeding bullets when You want to, yes? That's the book on You, isn't it? Jesus, save me. Please, holler at your boy, soften my enemies, bribe the devil. Halt my crucifixion.

Yes, when Gilbert, full birth certificate name Gilbert Ernst Chevalier, before his childhood friends shortened his name to Gil and his New York City friends spiced it up to Gil the Voodoo Child, aka Kid Haiti, aka Coconut Head, aka Le Walking Heartbreak, aka Le Green-eyed Nigger, aka Frenchie, aka That Kraut Nigga, aka Curly Hair Boy, and before his football friends called him Le Savior, aka Black Jesus, aka Orfeu Negro, the last one came from a mouth-watering Brazilian beauty on a toe-curling happy night in Belo Horizonte that nursed his wet dreams for years all the way to this, his dying day, when Gilbert saw death, his death, coming, he was bewildered and tried to reconnect with God, which was not easy since during his brief, wondrous life he felt and lived like a god among men. Americans call the sport soccer, the rest of the world calls it football, and therein lies the rub, the disconnection at the heart of the schizophrenic All-American life of Gilbert Chevalier. When football fans in the world outside America say the word, football becomes mystical, part child's play, part religion, a dreamy pleasure, an enchantment, the word *football* itself becomes an incantation, a magical theater of feet and ball, gravity and grass, head, hips, torso, and speed and balance, most unnatural combinations, but these skills have fascinated the world since the sport's conception in China in the fourth century Before Christ, and definitely since it's been popularized by England via its empire, such skills, timing, and intelligence seem otherworldly, full of bursts of supernatural grace. For a species that uses hand-eye coordination for practically everything it does every second of every single day, football sounds awkward and alien, therefore a skilled footballer moves through the world differently and is perceived like a stranger, part primitive, part demigod. Football players can afford to be average-looking men and women of varying heights and builds, but they are capable of feats with their feet that no one should have time to develop, or be blessed with, oh those lucky bastards, footballers. Fans often look at football players with a fervid awe. Why them and not me? Why are my feet useful merely for ambulating my body to and fro while footballers can play with their feet and a ball and thrill crowds to no end? How can they bend space and time and opponents with such efficient speed and delicacy and score goals, moving the ball past goalkeepers from odd angles despite the brutish ferocity of defenders? Why did God or the gods or Mother Nature bless only a few of us on this planet with those wildly entertaining powers? Why not me, God? Gil was born with the gift of footballing and so many other blessings to enjoy that he never found time to question them. Well, until today, his death day. As is customary for the exponentially gifted among us, Gilbert Chevalier's gifts for playing football, not soccer, with its robotic evocation of socks and fouls, but football, poetic, sensual, democratic football, earned him triumph and glory and even a brief siesta on top of the world. The world! Not a world, THE world, but it wasn't the entire world, was it? He didn't end any wars, cure diseases, or give birth, hell, he didn't even bring peace to Haiti, not between Haitians or between Haiti and the United States of America, its mighty frenemy, or did he? It's among the questions at the heart of this tale of a gifted young man and the demands of his passions, his family, his politics, and all the things he couldn't control but felt satisfying and overwhelmingly important, that one afternoon in Brazil, for example, sure felt ecstatic to Gilbert Chevalier and everyone who witnessed it or followed it on the radio or got secondhand word of his performance on the steamy pitch of the Mineirão in Belo Horizonte, for World Cup football touches everyone in the world, whether they want it to or not, whether their nation played in it or did not, whether they even liked football or not, were good at it or never tried to kick a damn football, indifference was hard to hang on to. What the hell is football? Why would someone try to be good at that? But even those skeptical souls would hear of Gilbert Chevalier, the magical Haitian, and if they didn't, if they merely saw him walking past a window of their restaurant in Manhattan, Barcelona, Port-au-Prince, or Belo, they sensed the boyish man with the commanding posture was exceptional, they knew he was special, and if they knew football they told him how much he meant to them, wherever he went in all the continents, the game against England had come to define him, protect him, gild him, until, abruptly, it didn't, an unmarked grave beckoned, he was on the verge of losing his life for another world, and the memory of his moment of glory and all the loving meaning attributed to it by thousands of strangers was slipping away, fading to near black as a firing squad stood a fraction of a second away from killing him, a slightly funny thing was happening inside him in this instant before his death, when he looked at all those black men brandishing big black machine guns filled with black bullets aimed at his skinny black body, just ten feet away, Gilbert Chevalier's life flashed before his eyes. The devil grew impatient. He hated this part of stealing souls like most people hated advertising. Sometimes the flashbacks happened after a person suffered a blow, or a heart attack, or a blow that triggered a heart attack, or the blow of a heart attack, or too much booze, or a heart attack triggered by too much booze, or sex, great sex, booze and heart-pounding sex, the best kind, yes, Gil Chevalier had had all types of sex, the heart-stopping kind in particular, his and his lovers' hearts stopped, in sync, he died, she died, they really did, die, resting in orgasmic peace, then, slowly, gingerly, his eyes opened, tenderly, his lover's eyes opened too, their breathing restored, softly, my god, woman, he'd whisper, voice scratching like sandpaper, I didn't know anyone could feel so sweet, how could you? How did you? Who made you!?! Oh we're good together, I'm keeping you in my life for sure, he'd continue, come here, sweet thing. We gonna die together. Let's die again?

But today, Gil will die for real. This day he is standing and shaking in place, facing a fate that his charm and hard-on couldn't sway, his fate is beyond his control, his goose is cooked, at this point he can't even stop himself from pissing in his pants, the stench of the dehydrated coward's pee rising from the dirt and burning his nostrils. His pounding heart ached. His memories bore down on him like boulders on a lost skier during an avalanche, there were a lot of good times, postcard images of a life filled with more blessings than blues, they were worth thousands of words, millions, billions of words, sometimes the images in Gilbert's head paused, and this sensation disgusted the devil. Love, his nemesis, ever so teasingly, caressed Gil on his death stand. It evoked a world of yearning and an ocean of tears and pleasures, and the feeling would coalesce into the image of the sweet pretty face of the only woman he ever, truly loved. Aurélie. Her name was Aurélie. The loving emotions the name aroused in him moved quickly from a caress to a bear hug, thunder bellowed in his chest, his mind became clear. Loving Aurélie was the most solid and true feeling he knew. Aurélie Picard. In his imagination she has grown to become his Rosebud and his Beatrice rolled into one. His savior and his own personal Orfeu Negro, and this day, seeing her face and hearing her voice and feeling her touch, one last time, one more time, till death made them part, was his dying wish. There were other women in the roll call of his life, in fact, there were mostly women, because Gilbert was a Chevalier, a very Haitian man, old school, *un homme à femme*, women were his leitmotif and *raison d'être*, his alarm clocks and metronomes, his masters and commanders, women like Elizabeth, the regal Nazi, Léa, the sultry American, a revolting woman, wrong in all the right ways, Nubia L'Insolente, *la brésilienne*, and sundry others.

Mais Aurélie, elle est mon dieu et ma déesse, he thought

in his final second. *Elle était ma Vierge et mon Saint Esprit.* Please forgive the blasphemy, God, You put her in my life, not me. Your grace and hers were the love of all loves for me. On this day, she is my dying wish, like the music of her voice and the taste of her belly button are the only thrills and moments of grace I wish for before ascending to Your heaven or down to hell, for hell is always a possibility, even for me, isn't it, God, You humorless bastard? The devil must be hovering around me right now like a chef sniffing a boiling soup. I see you, devil. You're not a football fan, are you? You probably like swimming. Or worse, baseball. Aurélie, wherever you are, baby, I love you and I miss you, and I didn't want to die before you, I don't want to die without you, and death fucking sucks cuz its unwanted embrace reminds me that you gave me the best hug I ever had. Knowing you made me whole, and without you I became a listless asshole, oh God, she was the One, wasn't she? We don't get too many women like that in our lives, do we? I blew it. I blew it. I blew it. Was it because I had too many women too easily and lost track and control of the only woman who was perfect for me? I didn't stop myself when the right one, *ma reine*, came along, God, You must hate me for my carelessness with such a blessing. Such a gift! Was it because of football? Or my family?

You must hate all of us who love football most of the time then. But that wouldn't be fair. For football is life. Love of football vs. the love of my life was not a fair fight. Not for me anyway.

But the worst thing about thinking about Aurélie and football for Gil during his last breath was feeling the heat of his passions flow through every cell of his sweaty, terrified body.

He saw her smile, framed by a halo of sunshine on an endless green field filled with goalposts and the sounds of whistles and cheers. She loved me as much as I loved her, didn't she, God? he thought, trying to unearth a doubt that didn't exist and never would. *Mais j'étais pas à la hauteur de son amour*, was I, God? I wanted to be. I really wanted to be. I tried my damnedest to hang on to her and us. Even in Brazil. Even in New York City, and You of all people know how difficult New York City temptations are for us Catholics. So I get it. I failed. We belonged to each other, it was a love between two Haitians that preceded colonialism, preceded the natives that named Haiti Ayiti, a love that was forged in the birth of the universe, billions of years ago, the Big Bang. Le Big Bang, *à l'haïtienne.* Yes, I can see us. Conceived by the Big Bang, we were a Big Bang. Even though, morally, in the moment, our love was also wrong. All wrong. All the wrongs. You see, I had responsibilities, a wife . . .

Please give me a stay of execution, God, and let me get out of this prison to go find her and my wife and make things right.

Gil wasn't even sure which woman he needed to beg for forgiveness, his wife or Aurélie. Or that maybe a woman wasn't at the root of his deadliest sin.

Can love of God overcome my vanity and save me from crucifixion this day, Jesus? Would the devil?

Can either one of you?

I refuse to accept that!

Fuck death!

Damn it, the devil now realized, love would save the day. But Gil won't see it coming.

Seigneur, I whispered, come on, Lord, please don't let me die today of all days and not here of all places, a dusty courtyard in the worst prison in the Caribbean, yes, God, You, the God of Catholics, Jews, Hindus, Buddhists, Sikhs, atheists, nonbelievers, and haters, devils and killers, and despots, all of us, all of us, I'm talking to You, our Lord and Savior, not the Dictator with the god complex who condemned me to death. I know You hate my arrogance, right? I'm among the most arrogant people You ever created. All professional athletes and artists are. Don't You see how stubborn we have to be to make our dreams and talents come true? *Oui, oui, je sais, suis un peu osé mais pourquoi pas?* Why not go to the highest authority? Ain't no atheists in foxholes.

And Gil, who has professed atheism to seduce a woman, was a lousy atheist. He wasn't much better at being a Catholic either, he'd be the first to admit. He was a lapsed Catholic. In other words, he was like just about every Catholic in two thousand years, ever since the first Catholics moved out of their parents' houses and stopped going to mass on Sundays. Away from his mother's pleading eyes, Gil was mediocre at practicing the faith. He held grudges for far too long, lusted too easily, and couldn't find a church to worship in if he was standing in a pew. He'd grown into a Catholic with a rap sheet that proved for the trillionth time that no man is worthy of fame. Yet, like most Haitians, he suffered a steady drumbeat of traumas from witnessing a lot of extreme misery and political violence and incompetence. He suffered the false assumption that he had extra credit with God, because, you know, it was pretty to think so.

You gotta face the facts, Gil, the devil whispered, your God is ironic and easily distracted.

Because God, if God exists, must listen to desperate prayers like yours by the trillions daily, He must certainly burst into laughter most of the time, like, you are kidding Me, right? Really, NOW you come to Me? Where were you, Gilbert, before shit hit the fan? Where were you when things were going swell and smelling sweet? When a thousand Brazilian women flashed you some leg? What did you do with the blessings that He had bestowed you? Did you see your glass as always half-full? What did you do for your brothers and sisters when you were healthy and prosperous and adored by strangers and relatives and friends to merit His consideration now that you're sick and scared and feeling a murderer's steel barrel press against your delicate cheekbones?

Yes, God seemed to have stopped listening to Gil Chevalier's prayers a long time ago. Bullshit, Jesus said, in Gil's right ear. But the devil's rap in Gil's left ear had momentum. Maybe God forgot about you since He made you a global celebrity against your will? Remember you were never supposed to play football in New York, much less go play in a World Cup, thinking no one would notice your broken promises to your father? Maybe Gil was doomed the minute he was born wealthy and handsome with incredible gifts for sports? Or later, when God made him marry a woman he didn't love and leave Haiti for the benefit of the family fortune? Even today, this dreaded day, Gil remembers with freshly boiled rage all those decisions that weren't his, but were necessary for the family. Today, the likely last day and instant of his life, he really wanted to play things cool, like he was made of diamond. He really did. He'd been working on looking unimpressed in impressive moments ever since he read Maurice Leblanc's *Arsène Lupin* novels as a child. He dreamed of growing up to become a gentleman thief, like Lupin, and he kinda did, he became a gentleman and a thief, not of jewels, but of rarer things, the hearts of women who saw him enter a room and those of every football fan who saw him play. For a long time, for far too long some would say, he was a giant man in a child's game. He never feared physical danger, like those moments when he faced the ire of defenders on a football field's penalty box, or rogue cops, or, more often than not, jealous boyfriends, when they had the goods on him and came barreling toward him with murder in their eyes. Come to think of it, the first time it happened he peed himself too and panicked like he was panicking today in front of the firing squad of Fort Dimanche. The first time may have been in 1949 or was that '55 in Spain or '70 in Miami? He'd been in jail for so long, tortured by the sameness of the horrible situation, the tiny cell, the absence of due process, the cruel silence of his jailers. He had lost track of time. Hot days and searing nights pummeled him with their withering and heavy constancy. They melted into each other and blurred over time, and time folded upon itself and speared clean through his sanity. He had forgotten what freedom and relief felt like, and, also, what freedom from yearning for relief from despair felt like. Can despair inhabit you so completely for so long that you become despair, like your name becomes Wretched Torment, and whatever names your parents and friends gave you were erased and replaced completely, wiped clean? Memories of the sweet breezes of good days gone by vanished from your heart, which was now shriveled to the meekness of a mouse.

I had virtues, didn't I, God? Gil cries to the heavens.

Yes, but bad luck is hard to explain, the skies replied.

Somewhere between his last cigarette and the impact of the first bullet against his purple single front tooth, his sins flashed before his eyes too. Why so many lowlights, God? he thought. Didn't You love me at all? Did You love me, at least a little bit? I loved You! Why do You hate me so?

In that instant, Gil remembered the first time he was blindsided by a hate he misread as love.

2

LES CHEVALIER OF THE CARIBBEAN

Gilbert's brother Jackie was a real peach. While facing his execution, Gil remembered everyone with love so strong the swell of affection might stop the dozens of bullets from imminently exploding his chest and head open. But the rose-colored-glasses moments of his life and times failed to help him forget things like the fact that his brother Jackie hated him enough to try to kill him all the time when they were kids. Like that time on the beach in Jacmel. It was even kind of funny.

Jackie: I bet you I can leap over that bed of broken rum and beer bottles from a running start and land safely into the sea.

Gil: Deal. Let's race.

Only during his second day in Hôpital General after barely surviving being stabbed in the lungs by broken bottles after failing to clear their lair did Gilbert Chevalier realize Jackie had stopped running the race and was grinning devilishly when Gil fell to his near doom. They were six years old.

Oh God, Jackie was such a shit, he recalled at his execution. Jackie knew me and pissed me off better than anyone else in the world. Even now, I don't want to die before him.

Can't let the asshole outlive me. He might go to heaven, and I might go straight to hell, but damn it, I have to live longer than him. He also knew me the longest. He knew me way back when we were sperm.

Jackie and Gilbert were born the exact same summer evening, a few minutes apart in the same compound in the Pétionville neighborhood of Port-au-Prince in 1924. Geminis through and through. Bastard brothers with the same father. By the hazards of fate, one of them was born a prince, the other a pauper.

Gilbert's mother gave birth to him in the largest bedroom on the top floor of a pink mansion lit, LIT, fire-hazard bright, by scented candles while being fussed over by a squadron of midwives and not one, but two of the finest doctors in Haiti. Jackie's mother gave birth to him on the floor of a maid's quarters with the help of the gardener whose first and only words to the newborn were *Tais toi*. Shut up.

Their mothers couldn't have been more different, though they were both striking, beautiful women. *Une noire et une mulâtre.* Like a song. Alice *la mulâtre,* in an uncommon twist, was one of the family's maids. Her caramel-colored face was sharply sculpted and frequently stretched by her jet-black long hair pulled into a bun. Her face sparkled with freckles that made her look like she possessed eternal youth and gaiety. Marie, *la noiraude reine de la maison,* had an imperial bearing and penetrating dark eyes with long wet lashes that mesmerized people and urged men and boys and some women to feel like they should kneel before her. Those dark eyes gave Gilbert a lifelong attraction to dangerous women who thrill and then try to break his heart into a million pieces. Except for Aurélie, her dark eyes gave Gil a sense of ownership, and they were filled with shiny and limitless affection, and faith in him, no sign of doubt, a fact that troubled him and also gave him the greatest joy.

Jackie and Gil's father, Thomas, was the same weak and careless man. He had a soft chin, flaccid morals, and a limp handshake. But he was wealthy and the worst kind of rich, a scion, born with mountains of money and assets that included an actual mountain in Hinche, a province of central Haiti. All he had to do with his life was protect the capital, live off the interest, and not have too many children to fritter that shit away. It was meant to last a couple of generations, but it would not. This is Haiti after all. What is supposed to be rarely is. Basically, Thomas Chevalier was a typical Caribbean-European aristocrat. Port-au-Prince might as well have been Aruba or Martinique or Jamaica to his kind, and indeed he had cousins bathing in family fortunes as old as Christopher Columbus all over the Caribbean and South America and Europe. His father's father came to Haiti a few decades earlier as a junior consul from Germany with burning ambition and one specific mission: to marry into a good Haitian family to help his compatriots circumvent the Haitian law barring foreigners from owning property in Haiti. Haitians hate foreigners with enduring passion. A reasonable legacy after centuries of being terrorized by colonialism, both hard (pre-1804) and soft (every day since January 1, 1804, and the fabled successful Haitian revolution against France). Haitians perceive all foreigners as once and future colonizers, a knee-jerk reflex from having rejected enslavement by Europe and somehow being branded evil for doing so. We even paid off France, the thirstiest of all colonizers of the Caribbean and Africa. We paid them $21 billion we didn't have to persuade them to resist the impulse of trying to recolonize us after we kicked Napoleon's ass. They removed their gunships from the port of Port-au-Prince once the checks cleared, but they stayed bitter and haughty. We stayed broke and twitchy. The Germans were slicker. We didn't see them coming. Gil's colonizing grandfather's mission was all too successful. He married shrewdly. She was a frizzy-haired and leggy chocolate goddess whose skeptical father couldn't say no to her desire for a sunburnt man who looked like he was bleeding from the searing heat of the ever-bright Caribbean sun. Grandpa Bernhard Merkel was gallant and shrewd enough to take his wife's family name, Chevalier, before raping and pillaging her country by diligently opening the door for Prussian industry to invade Haiti while he skimmed sizable pieces of the action. He built a huge fortune for his family and the fatherland and had one son, a boy who grew up to love the privileges of being a white-looking Haitian more than he cared about fellow Haitians, a malevolent indifference that was all too common since 1492 and the arrival of Spanish settlers.

With a passion for beautiful things, people, and places, the scion quickly became the most Haitian Prussian ever. Graceful, sweet, and crass, depending on his moods, Papa slept with every remotely attractive woman or girl from Port-au-Prince to Cap Haïtien to Port Salut. As long as he didn't get anyone pregnant, and somehow, he avoided doing so for far longer than most philanderers, Grandfather looked the other way. But Grandpa died after his skull got crushed by a falling coconut during an afternoon nap under a tree in his compound in Kenscoff, so he didn't get to see his son, my father, get two women pregnant at the same time. Once aware of her husband's transgression, *Maman* brought permanent arctic chill to their marital bed in the middle of the Caribbean Ocean. The two women may very well have gotten pregnant the same day, since Father abhorred free time and had no other hobbies, other than his football team, and even that was something he won after a buddy bet him he couldn't seduce the nubile wife of a star player.

Gilbert wonders if he grew up to become a relatively prudish Haitian because of subconscious disgust for his handsy father. We'll never know that one for sure, but we do know two of his father's lovers gave birth to babies on the same evening in 1924 while he was outside pacing and smoking in the vast garden separating the big house and the outhouse, I mean the servants' quarters. Very tall and lean, with an aquiline face and pasty skin that seemed incapable of tanning, Thomas Chevalier, *mon père*, looked like a regal asshole. He chain-smoked and paced and waited for his two sons' births in the vast and elaborate garden, one with hedges designed to copy Versailles itself, separating the servants' quarters where his girlfriend, the maid, lived, and the big gingerbread pink mansion where he lived with his wife, my mother. His best friend, Gaston, waved glasses of rum at him, and Thomas drank them in big gulps, but he never took a seat on the bench. The wait was killing him. He wanted a boy and a girl, one child to inherit and run the business and the other to love him unconditionally.

I don't know which baby our father held first in his arms that night, Jackie or me, Gil reminisced. I do know which baby he bounced on his knee in his study during the period when the baby was restless and thirsty for affection. I do know which boy he confided in as a friend when he told me he would begin to take the family business as seriously as possible for he did not want to leave Mother and me with less wealth than his father left him. And I can tell you which baby he greeted most formally whenever they shared the same room, which happened rarely, you see, because the compound we lived in was vast and located on a hilltop. The family mansion was not even its central building, tucked away as it was in a forest of hydrangeas, the cool scent of which became everyone's favorite, permanent perfume.

On top of being an illegitimate child hated by the mistress of the compound and all who curried her favor, Jackie had the misfortune of being ugly and bookish and not good at sports. Oh, how I envied his way with words. Me, the main thing I had going for me early on was beauty. By all accounts, especially those of women of all ages, I looked good, like a godling, *a ne plus ultra* of African and Northern European genes. My body hoarded the winnings of a successful *métissage*, a mixing of European, Native American, and African features that was perfected beyond the highest Caribbean standards, which are nothing to scoff at. I supposedly grew into a caramel Adonis, benefitting also from an education that gave me fluency in about five languages, French, Spanish, English, German, and the greatest and most celebrated language of them all, seduction. I had a great head of curly hair, fleshy lips, and clear eyes that seemed to change to any color a woman desired to see her reflection and feel transported to an exotic world. Jackie may have been an inch or so taller than me, but the poor thing didn't inherit my naturally commanding posture. He did not make men want to stand up and salute him when he entered a room. He did not inspire grown women and young girls to beg for an approving glance from his brown-green eyes, like I did. Jackie's eyes, the girls said, were the wrong shades of green, inhuman. You look like a zombie, the sister or best friend of my girlfriend of the moment would inevitably say to him during our double dates. We both had our father's lean athletic physique, but Jackie's came with a hunch. Is that the reason Jackie hated me?

I hate you, he said, whenever we played a game, and that's all we did, play games, which he won, he always won, even, occasionally, at basketball and ping-pong, I didn't mind, for he was my best friend, he needed to beat the shit out of me in everything we competed at, and I loved him anyway, always, so whenever we finished playing and he said the same thing, I hate you, Gil. I really do. I thought the smile on his face meant he was kidding.

I went to a posh school, St. Louis, one of the finest and oldest in Port-au-Prince, founded by our second president, the only one in Haitian history whose passion for education and serving common Haitians was greater than his love of himself. Jackie was home-schooled by his secretly deeply literate mother. My birthday parties featured clowns and bands and, when I turned eleven, an eleven-gun salute by soldiers under the command of a family friend, General Michael Clervoix, who was rumored to have replaced my father in the marital bed. Jackie's birthday parties were sad affairs, held inside his little room with me, his mom, the gardener, and a couple of other slaves' kids, er, servants' kids, the ones we played football with. Every other year or so, Father would transgress Mother's rules and visit Jackie's birthday party. He would grin mischievously at me and gaze tenderly at Jackie and his mother while playing the wall in a poor attempt at easing the heavy tension his presence caused. He plied Jackie with books as gifts. It was the strangest thing. Even though I was barely able to sneak Jackie inside the big house much, Father somehow heard about how much Jackie loved reading, and slowly but surely a lot of his favorite books made their way to Jackie. First they filled up his bedroom, forming towers that began from the floor and reached the ceiling to the point where it became dangerous to lean against the spots where the walls were supposed to be, obscuring even the beautiful poster of the Eiffel Tower I gave Jackie for his birthday, sparking his travel lust. Jackie dreamed of moving to Paris. Not me. I was fine with my life in Haiti. Papa and his friends saw me conquering the world. First, they had me winning everything of value in Haiti, leading its greatest industries, maybe the presidency of the republic, before settling down with the best and brightest of its wellborn girls, a lightskin doctor, of course, but not too light and definitely with big hair. Pretty and demure. A good girl. But only on the surface, you know what I'm sayin'? they'd joke. Then they saw me charming my way to the finest things and people elsewhere in the West, especially the U.S., Europe, a diamond mine or two in Africa. Never Asia. You never want to live long in a place where you look *that* different from the locals, Papa explained, unironically. The adventure's not worth it after five minutes.

I can't explain why, but fame and globetrotting held little interest for me, though everyone expected it to. Face it, Gilbert, you're destined to conquer the world, Jackie said, with, now that I think of it, quite a bit of sarcasm. You're going to become our hero, like Ulysses.

We were playing chess in his front yard. Homework shouldn't have had to wait, oh but it did.

Who?

Ulysses, you know, the hero of Homer's *Odyssey*, the epic poem of a man who just had to go wander the earth, even though his kingdom, the only place he truly belonged in the world, was on his island home, Ithaca, with the love of his life, Penelope.

Why do you believe I have to leave Haiti? Check. You're the one with the wild literary imagination.

True. But my life is pretty interesting as it is. Look around you. With all these books, I have the world in the palm of my hands. Check.

Shit, I thought I had him pegged. Not only did he effectively counter my attack, his counterattack was sharp. My queen and king were caught in a fork by his knight. Fucking knights. I hate them.

Oops.

Jackie smiled that enigmatic smile of his after I fake-sneezed and knocked the board down.

I have to go, I said. It's time for the football game.

I know.

I'll be back.

I know.

3

HAITIAN FOOTBALL SONG

On football game days, we went down to our house in a beautiful neighborhood of central Port-au-Prince called Bois Verna. The neighborhood was lined with thick trees and wonderful cooling shade. My father loved football, and, after acquiring a team, Aigle Noir, he built the team's clubhouse right next to our house in Bois Verna. After changing into the uniform, bright red shorts and white shirts, making us look super-heroic, I joined the team for our pregame meal, sitting next to my man Jeremy Kahn. Jeremy was my wingman in most things, but especially on the football pitch. He kicked crosses that often made the ball take high, graceful arcs before dropping immaculately at an angle I could hunt it down to break down a defense and score goals. I had asthma as a kid and wasn't allowed to play football for a few years, the saddest period of my life before my current life on death row. After my uncle George discovered a recipe for a cure for asthma called soursop, I started playing football with gusto, like my life depended on it. My passion would frighten some, but I couldn't help myself. Scoring goals in a football game felt as amazing as illicit sex to me. The feeling was irrepressible. So many games ended in 0–0 draws. You savored goals deeply because you never knew which game and goal could be your last for a while. My late start in the game left me with limited skills, but I seemed to have been born with the gift of deft first touch of the ball however it came at me, a striker's most valuable skill. I wasn't one of those players who could perform fancy dribbles and tricks with the ball at my feet, but I had a knack for corralling that damn thing and making it do one thing, one fucking thing, particularly well: fly past a goalkeeper and into the net. The gift revolved around running down the ball wherever else Jeremy or the opposite winger launched it into the box, and I would flick, kick, nudge, hand-job, stab, caress, beg, scream, curse, squeal, whatever it took, to bend the ball to my will and field of control, which was considerable since I had long limbs, a small waist, and broad shoulders, then I'd move the ball around a defender, or through defenders, if necessary, a seemingly magical trick that involved a great deal of pulling, scratching, grabbing, punching, elbowing, acting, grunting, and swiftness, lots of that, to kick, roll, French kiss, or head the ball past the goalkeeper, who was often rushing at me with deadly intent, for the penalty box was his kingdom, and I was a thief with an eye on the crown jewels, getting the ball across the goal line into the net. I poached the ball for goals. My God, I was good at it. My body would grow, stretch, push, or just plain contort to whatever form needed to get my right or left foot or stomach or neck or chest or head, especially my head, on that damn ball. I hated the football. I hated how much my happiness depended on how well I touched it and got rid of it. Strikers, a football team's principal scorers, don't get to touch the ball all that much during a typical football match, unlike, say, midfielders. In fact, much of our effectiveness, or lack thereof, depended on how good our initial touch of a ball was, how well we seduced that little black-and-white bastard after our teammates desperately sent it to us past walls of defenders.

My favorite passes came from the heavens. I could carve out space around big, beefy defenders in the dirt, or manhandle or fly over little defenders to get to it. Like my life depended on it. Always. People often asked me, Why did you play the game *so hard*, Gil? I would shrug. I had no idea there could be another way to play, a *softer* way. What the hell was that? Goals in football were exceedingly difficult to procure while everything else that most men valued—money, women, cool—came to me relatively easily. Football was a fickle lover that I could never completely please or certainly not come close to controlling, but I could approximate control, however briefly, and that in itself stirred my passions and those of crowds. Different vantage points, but we both hoped for the volcanic thrill of witnessing me bury a ball in the back of the net. When the net fluttered after the ball's penetration, ecstatic gasps rose from half of the crowd and disgusted moans came from the other half of the crowd, fans of the desecrated team. I loved how my mouth foamed, and my heart thundered, and I screamed whenever the opportunity came, and then, and then, completion.

Goooooooooooooaaaaaal.

In Haiti, we played foot on dirt pitches, I hated that too, I mean, come on, we lived on the largest island of the Caribbean, a verdant and gorgeous patch of blue-green earth surrounded by azure blue ocean waters, with a robust rainy season and mild dry season, but we couldn't find a grassy fucking knoll to play football, our great undying pastime?

Pardon my foul mouth. I picked up the habit during my time living in New York City. Yes, I lived in New York City, that big, glitzy jewel of American life. I'll tell you about it later.

Well-timed bursts of foul language were useful, I was told by Miles Davis, my first friend and roommate. Miles and his cousin Ron taught me the codes of cool as we roamed Harlem. One of them was that well-timed profanities livened any conversation and thrilled and seduced. It was also the best tool to lighten my French accent when I got to America and needed to smoothly assimilate that segregated, bustling, gigantic *bouillon*, where natives preferred people they considered alien to be a little risqué. African Americans were masters of ably shuttling between formality and vulgarity with flair. I didn't care about American interracial gamesmanship. I'm Haitian. Black, white, Latin, Native American, Gallic, Guinean, Beninois, American basically, *de souche, quoi*, if you want to sniff inside my DNA. But Haitian was enough. Captured it all. The good, the bad, and the chaotic. Thank you very much. We are the world. We are whatever we want to be. Today, I may be fucked up on death row in the worst country run by the worst government in the world, but scoffing at death is what Haitians do best. It's our birthright. Fuck death and fuck you. What do YOU do about death? Deny it. Hide from it. Tell yourself you're going to live forever? Not us. Our arrogance hits different. We absorb the greatest amount of assholery and shrug, like, that's how hard you can punch me in the face with my arms tied behind my back, life? That's your best tease, death? Fuck you!

Anyway, back to football, *mon amour*. I could scratch and claw with the meanest defensive ogres in the world to reach that ball, even when it came fast and hard like a bowling ball, but when the ball came from high passes, crosses or even chips, those were my shit. They played to my great height and stubborn, dexterous head. Diving headers were my signature move. I was ambidextrous with my feet, though. But for headers, I'm rabid. I'd jump and go completely airborne, body horizontal to the ground, and remain airborne for as long as necessary to find a way to head the ball into the net. Some fans called me Super-Haitian, like the popular new comic book superhero, Superman. I suppose I looked graceful in flight. But there was often nothing graceful about my landings, sometimes face-first in the dirt.

During the twenty-minute walk downtown to Parc Le Conte for the game, my teammates and I tried to walk under the giant almond trees for shelter from the exhaustively hot late afternoon sun, which was almost as devastating as the noon sun. We distracted ourselves, about girls, the future of the World Cup, and we whispered about our injuries, real or feared. There was occasional talk of the wars in Europe and Asia, but we kept those asides mercifully brief. Haiti knows war too well. We are perpetually at war against colonialists inside and outside the country. The 1940s were an interlude of peace. Some of us itched to make gas chamber jokes for what we were going to do to our opponents, but knew it was too soon. Our peace was too fragile for us to get cocky about the savagery of wars.

Concentrated, with sandals click-clacking, I'd roll my head from side to side to crack my neck, keep my breathing steady, and check to make sure my spine, my entire upper body, felt supple and ready to bend, elongate, or twist, so my feet or head or ears could seize and save the day when called upon. Like boxers we were, all but punching the air to loosen our arms, when it was our legs and feet and hearts that would betray us or deliver glory, sometimes in the same game, play, or minute.

That evening, under a full white moon, we lost the championship game after I missed a penalty kick at the end of the game. I missed the kick before I even kicked it. Shashou, Racing's goalkeeper, had upset me with his annoying stalling tactics after I set the ball up for my kick. It was a big game, the crowd for that day's game swelled to a few thousand. They all seemed to stand in the mouth of the goal with Shashou and his broad shoulders and round bald head. I watched him lick his lips and talk shit while rocking side to side to taunt me.

You not getting the ball past me, son, he said. The goal is tighter than your mother. Trust me, I know.

And my temper flared, like an out-of-body experience. The city seemed to be melting around me *and* inside me. My arms felt watery then stiff with sweat and anger. My shirt clung to my drenched torso like a second skin. I felt especially hot under the collar because the foul that triggered the penalty was especially dirty. Motherfucking Shashou had punched me in the head as I went for the ball for a goal. You don't punch people in the head, man. I kicked my penalty into the stands to distract him and lunged the entire distance to the goal to wrap my hands around his meaty neck and then pound the shit out of his face. It felt so good. Who's laughing now? I'd lost my professionalism, my cool, my head, and the championship to a clever old dude's gamesmanship, like the kid I was. There was no reason at work in this situation save for the emotions of a teenager's spasm of idiocy and testosterone.

No one spoke to me after my absurdly terrible game and behavior. Not even our coach, Tonton Gregoire, a jovial stoic if there ever was one. Jeremy barely managed to whisper a few kind words in my ear as I sat on a stool in front of my locker still numb with rage for no damn reason—the missed penalty, the frustration I caused my team, and the money in bonuses I cost my teammates were far from my mind, until suddenly, they were all I could think of. Guilt shrouded me.

What will Father Sidney make of this mistake of mine at confession on Wednesday?

Teammates didn't steer clear of me out of sympathy or anger. I was the boss's son. They avoided me because they didn't know how the boss would react to my fuckup. They didn't want to be close to me and become collateral damage if things got nasty.

Good, you've showered.

It was Dad's voice, strangely chipper. I looked up. Dad wore his usual white suit, pants, espadrilles, and sucked on a cigar. Next to him stood a German couple. How did I know they were German and not Dutch or Swiss or French, like so many whites in Haiti? You just know. The husband looked like he could play a judge in a movie. I mean, he had wisps of blond hair that were disappearing fast, broad shoulders, wore an expensive dark suit, a monocle, and stared unblinkingly at me with cold blue eyes. His wife was sad-eyed and plain, though her bust was impressive enough that my father could barely keep his eyes off it. The couple had two fair-haired daughters in tow. I found the way the oldest daughter, the ginger-haired one, held on, no, gripped her father's arm, touching. Daddy's little girl. I'm fond of them.

Her blue eyes were clear and moist. They nursed mine gently throughout dinner. I felt denuded by those eyes. A thrilling and slightly frightening feeling. We were at Panorama, a restaurant for big shots, up in the hills of Kenscoff. The food was so-so. The restaurant's best feature was the, yes, panoramic view of Port-au-Prince, framed by a sea of puffy white clouds floating about like cotton candy, close to the touch. My father said something about how the Schattenhams were old friends of the family from back in Prussia, and that they would be staying with us for a few months for a bit of respite from all the unpleasantness of the war.

What war? I said, aren't the Americans all gone?

I'm talking about the war in Europe, Gilbert, Papa said.

The Germans looked at Dad, like, what other war exists or has ever existed? They had no idea that Haiti had been fighting an occasionally hot but perpetually cold war against the United States, its overbearing and overweening northern neighbor, more or less since both countries came into existence in the late eighteenth century. We'd won the last conflagration, only after twenty years of resistance to an American occupation of our economy by a battalion of marines. Our nation was tired. Dad was exhausted, jumpy, like most Haitians who had lived through the Occupation. They feared the Americans would return one way or the other, and this time they'd be stronger and tougher to beat. Colonial powers always returned. They can't help it. Empires are not gracious losers.

The war against the American Occupation raged through most of my childhood, from 1915 to 1934. That war was a drag, and fifteen years after the last American tank left Haiti, most Haitians were still mad that the Americans had been here in the first place. In the same way we forever hated France, the first colonial power we beat to win freedoms we shouldn't have had to fight to gain. Fighting the world's richest, oldest, and largest armies from our Caribbean hamlet with scant resources at our disposal other than rage and pride left us permanently twitchy. Most Haitian men slept with one eye open and a shotgun under their arms, literally and intellectually, fearing the Yankees' treacherous return. *Et les gaulois aussi*, though we also knew they never left. French culture was alive and well in the mores and ways of the Haitian bourgeoisie, spiked with creole to charm the peasants. My father, however, was not one of those proud, conquest-phobic Haitians. He was born a double agent and never changed. He was profoundly American about that, too. I may be Haitian by nationality and charm, he often said, but I'm European and American when it comes to money: austere on the surface, greedy at heart. A true Puritan. Purely selfish.

In fact, the only time in my life I had ever seen Papa cry was the day in 1934 when we stood on the quai of Port-au-Prince, along with throngs of other Haitians, and watched the American troops take their trucks, green fatigues, rolled up red, white, and blue flags, and other possessions and board ships to take permanent leave of Haiti at the end of the Occupation. The Americans, squinting and weathered, looked defeated, although it was hard to ascertain exactly how we finally beat them. From what I came to later understand about how history was recorded, if it's written in English, Haitians will always look bad, whether we escaped American bullying or not. More perniciously, America never admits to losing wars. Its wars merely end. Since they remained powerful and wealthy, and Haiti, like many former conquests, remained underdeveloped and forlorn, American historians had a point.

As I prepare to die this morning, I struggle to remember that some corners of the world, especially in America, would remember me fondly. After all, once upon a time, I gave the Americans their greatest moment on a world stage. Of course, the man I was then, that Gilbert Chevalier, was a mere entertainer, a sportsman, not in just any sport, but the world's most beloved sport, but that celebrated man had precious little to do with the person I was inside. In my heart, I was a temperamental Catholic boy whose first wife was going to be a pretty Nazi that I couldn't make happy.

4

NAZI LOVE

Papa cried today. It didn't seem like a crying day in Haiti, but I was too young to know better. I didn't yet know that many days, dare I say most days, after a certain age, are crying days. The day I saw my father cry for the first time feels like yesterday, or maybe it was thirty years ago, my memory has been dodgy since I've been living in a dungeon on death row. But the thought of my father in tears always made me cry, and I'm crying right now, for death was invading my body. It's been a while since I cried, but in the face of death's cold caress, what else was left to do? I've lost track of time, since our country has one unblinking season. Really not funny, God. After countless years of imprisonment without judgment, now, finally, I'm facing a firing squad, my confessions compel me to tell You about the day my father cried. In fact, I'm peeing myself as I tell this story to You, Jesus, the Holy Ghost, or Whom It May Concern, because my body is failing me after all these years of malnutrition and fear. For whatever reason, my mind is hanging in there, so please hear my prayer, God. I never got to be a father. Fathers should never have to bury their sons.

I was small the day I saw Papa cry. I was standing by his

side, not taller than his waist. Maybe about nine years old. His big hands swallowed mine. It was morning, early enough for a whiff of a chill to float in the air. His hand was soft with defeat. We stood on the edge of the port of Port-au-Prince, blue-green waters ten feet below us, swaying prettily. We watched our compatriots jeer a parade of retreating American soldiers as they clambered onto their warships for a one-way trip back home. The brave souls among them even threw a stone or can or potato at the tired Yankees. Not that we were alone in hating these men; this was the closest thing to a parade they would ever receive for having spent two decades raping and pillaging Haiti. They were successful but not permanently so, the losers. Papa, however, wept openly, loudly, for them, which struck me as strange. I was shaken. Fathers weren't supposed to cry, certainly not my all-powerful, all-knowing, captain of industry *père*. I remember solemnly swearing to myself I would do whatever I could in the future to make sure this man, my hero, for better or for worse, would never shed another tear and look so weak again. My mistake, however, was to think my father was weeping for the departing imperialists.

I'm crying for myself, *mon chéri*, Papa said, to my sad, inquiring eyes. I'm crying for us. These men, these sons of bitches, as they like to call themselves, these incredibly clumsy oafs who your countrymen hate so lustily, these men were our meal tickets, son. We're watching a very big chunk of the family fortune leave Haiti right now. We overcharged them for everything for twenty years! It was beautiful. Rents, mortgages, gas, food, laundry, electricity, beach access. Everything, and they paid the exorbitant charges without blinking and on time! When was the last time you saw a Haitian be on time for anything? These gullible wealthy fools were prompt with payments. You just had to appear humble and grateful and efficient to them. Nobody loves gratitude more than Americans. *C'est une addiction chez eux. Pas si méchant que ça. C'est comme tout le monde, je suppose. Mais chez eux, c'était drôlement lucratif.* Now they're gone. We're fucked.

Fucked?

Never mind, son. Let's just say I don't know how the family business will survive without the American Occupation and their torrents of dollars.

You'll figure it out, Papa, I said, glad money was his only worry. I was young. I didn't know then what I would learn later. Among most adults, money is the only worry.

We'll figure it out, he said, hugging me to his thigh, a twinkle returning to his eyes.

As it turned out, the lean years came, they came swiftly, and they were tough. Within a decade, we were broke, gradually then completely. Like tumbleweed drifting loosely but swiftly off a cliff.

I was around eighteen the day of that football game when my father asked me to save the day and help undo all his suffering after the end of the American Occupation. I honestly thought they would never leave, Father said, of the Americans and their economy-inflating Occupation. But they did, and the profits from those days are gone. Our businesses are barely staying afloat. I need your help, he said.

Father and I were standing closely in his study. I'm feeling like a man now, looking like one too. The forties had been unkind to Papa, like aging can be to all men. Whispering, ostensibly so as not to wake our guests, though the house, like the room, was large enough that no one could hear us. The whispering was meant to impress me with the gravity of the situation, and what Father was about to ask of me. It's deep into the night. A baggy silver moon smirked high up in the black sky, drenching the room with light through its large, floor-to-ceiling windows. At first I half-listened to him. I couldn't wait for him to finish. I'd promised Elizabeth, our sexy new houseguest from Germany, that I'd visit her with a nightcap.

. . . you marry Elizabeth.

What?!!!

Papa's tone of voice went flat. His heart wasn't in this. Every other part of him was, though. Listen, Gilbert, I'm going to be completely transparent with you, he said. Our visiting Schattenhams are not the nicest people. My grandfather was close to Christian Schattenham, a priest, back in Munich, turn of the century. Noble man. Good times. A different Germany. But these are Christian's less-high-minded cousins. They are Nazis. Klaus, with the monocle, was so high up in the Third Reich, they nicknamed him Hitler's Sphincter. He personally oversaw the killing of thousands of Jews and the looting of millions of dollars of their assets. As the Reich fell, he spirited most of it out of Germany and Poland and God knows where else, to Switzerland and other safe havens around the world. Now that most of his colleagues in the Reich who escaped the war tribunals have scattered around hideouts in South America, he figured he'd be more clever by half and hide his wealth and family in a less obvious country in the region. Haiti, our pearl of the Caribbean.

Jesus, Father, we should be turning him in, not harboring him.

In due time, son.

And what does this have to do with me and his daughter? Elizabeth's a nice girl and all, soft on the eyes with a nice touch of wickedness in the lips, but marriage? That's a tad bit premature, no, Papa?

Papa batted away my attempt at levity.

Listen, this is not a game. I won't allow you to blow up this deal like that football match. This. Is. Not. A. Game. *Je ne rigole pas, chéri.* I don't want Klaus's dirty money either. We're going to have to answer to God for that. But the Nazi money will save our business. Our business needs saving to ensure your great-grandchildren never have to work a day in their lives.

Dad, what's in it for me?

He seemed too determined to dissuade, so I might as well switch tactics and negotiate some fun for me out of the situation. It's nice to be needed.

Never having to work a day in your life and passing the privilege of the same lifestyle to your children and grandchildren.

Yes, Dad, I get that. But what's in it for me right now?

Father relaxed and pulled out a cigar and lit it.

Oh, so we're negotiating, are we?

New York City, I said. I marry this girl, so her father can funnel his Holocaust funds into our pockets, and you let me go to university in New York. I'll learn accounting or something, but I'll get to enjoy a little freedom after surrendering my bachelorhood to Chevalier Inc.

What are you talking about?

If you knew him as well as I knew him, you could hear him losing his cool.

Haiti has good universities, he said.

I just want to go to live in another country for a few years, I said. I just want to see how America works. We hate them so much it'll be good to know the enemy from the inside. Besides, living there will improve my English. The business will benefit from it all in the long run, no?

Freedom. I wanted to be free. But I couldn't tell Father that. He was closing a coffin on my youth, and I was suffocating, panicking, freaking out. I had to get off that damn island. Get some air. Just for a bit. America. Give me a last gasp of freedom in the land of the free.

After university, you'll come right back to Haiti to help me run the business? Papa said.

After university, I'll come straight back to Haiti to help you run the business. Papa took a deep puff of his cigar. His face then broke into a broad smile.

No more football.

What?

You heard me.

Why not? I stammered.

It's a poor man's sport. You're not temperamentally built for it. You're a businessman now, a leader, an investor. You are learning the first rule of family leadership.

I was crestfallen.

Which is?

You become a great leader only by sacrificing something dear to you. In the old days, I'd ask you to cut off a finger or something. I'm letting you off easy.

I would later learn this was the moment I was supposed to pause, take a moment, and stall the force of Father's argument until I found some wiggle room in it. Instead, in the moment, I assented, shakily.

D'accord, I said, wondering what fun he had sacrificed in the nearly twenty years I'd known him.

By the shadow of sadness I glimpsed on his face as I walked out of the room, I suspect he was going through the memories of his sacrifices at the altar of the family fortune. I hoped forcing me to marry a girl not of my own choosing was now on top of that list.

Meanwhile, on the other side of the pink mansion that evening, a disturbingly similar discussion was taking place in German in a much smaller room with smaller windows.

Let me get this straight, Father, Elizabeth said.

The girl was skinny but stout. Her thin pink lips and piercing eyes gave her face power that her slight frame lacked. She sat on a bed, feet crossed at the ankles, still in her prim white dress. Her parents stood before her. Her mom clutched her own right elbow. Her father kept his hands in pockets and stared at the ground.

We have no money, thanks to those lying and thieving bankers in Geneva. And now you want me to marry this boy I just met—who might be related to us by blood, by the way—because his family believes we have money we don't have to invest in their bankrupt business in this tropical hellhole. And you hope this marriage will help the world forget or forgive the fact that I'm the daughter of a leader of the most repugnant people earth has ever seen: Nazis.

Exactly, her mother, Bertha, said.

Father, you're really on board with this madness?

Klaus Schattenham paused just long enough before answering to indicate to Elizabeth that no, he was not on board, but he'd been following foul orders without questioning them for so long now that he did not know how to do otherwise.

It's the right thing to do for our family, he said.

It's not like you have to have sex with him, Bertha said.

Klaus winced.

By the time they realize we have no money, Bertha continued, Klaus's know-how will have pumped their businesses back to life. We'll then move on to Venezuela. You'll get to enjoy a comfortable life wherever you want, with whomever you want.

I want to go back home.

That won't be possible for a while, my sweet.

But you told me our trip here was a temporary retreat, the young girl said, meekly.

Her father put an arm around his wife and pulled her close to him with a heavy sigh. He needed the support. In a voice more frail than any teenage girl's, he said, I lied. I'm sorry.

The room seemed to grow darker, save for candlelight and the shimmer of moonlight that gave a saintly glow to a confused girl's white dress.

The next afternoon Gilbert Chevalier walked out of his schoolyard, and, like the big child he was, thinking about fun, not marriage. I had forgotten about that conversation with Father like it had been a bad dream. I was with a few buddies. It was a Monday. The weather clearly called for a romp at the beach. Which beach? Carrefour seemed like a good call. Jeremy knew some girls there. The second I walked through the school's gates, my senses exploded and lost all contact with the world. I couldn't hear, touch, smell, and could barely see anything beyond the beautiful vision in front of me. The guys asked what was wrong. Their voices sounded distant. I couldn't remember her name at that instant, but her face gave me an unprecedented shock. She was standing in front of the car with Frantz, my driver. She was a vision. Blond ringlets cascading to her pert breasts, shiny, welcoming eyes, lean body, bare, muscular arms, and shoulders that suggested a confidence and power I somehow missed the night before. I slowed my pace, as I found myself rushing toward her, then I picked my jaw up off the ground. My heart beat too fast. Maybe she heard its pounding through the noise of downtown Port-au-Prince and liked it. She smiled sweetly at me.

Wie geht es Ihnen? she said.

Quoi? I said.

Was? she said.

Merde.

The mousy Nazi of the previous night had transformed into a Teutonic angel. But, damn, I had to seduce her into marrying me to save my family fortune, but she couldn't speak or understand my French, and I didn't speak German that well. In the backseat of the car, I told Frantz to take us straight to the beach. Not the swell one in Carrefour, but a more discreet beach, up the National. The last thing I wanted to do was give my buddies a chance to hit on her before I figured out how to get around our language barrier. At the sight of the majestic Matheux mountains, I could see awe in her eyes and the parting of her lips. Haiti was beginning to impress her, and I was falling in love with her just for that. The hitch was, I had no idea how to communicate the sentiment besides smiling.

At the beach, hints of the faded oranges of dusk rose in the distance. Elizabeth struggled to walk on the hotel's courtyard gravel in her red sandals. I expected her to be slightly repulsed by the lobby we walked through. Nice, spacious, the Spanish villa style was meant to channel Caribbean breezes and quick check-ins. I liked it, but I figured the hotel was shabby compared with the hotels she saw growing up in Munich. She took it all in with wonder, her sandals slapping the marble floor in applause. Her eyes eventually settled on the white-crested waves roaring outside. She walked toward the ocean as if in a trance. I nodded to the concierge that she was with me. He nodded solemnly back like he knew I'd pay for everything on my way out, or my father would. By the time I caught up to her on the beach, she held her sandals in her hands, her bare feet buried in the sand. Eyes closed, head tilted toward the heavens, she stood at the edge of the ocean and seemed to be trying to draw all that is good and beautiful about Haiti and its place in the center of the Caribbean Sea into her lithe, pale body. The people are even better than the ocean views, I whispered in her ear, close enough for my five o'clock shadow to graze her cheek.

She looked at me from the corner of her eyes and smiled before playfully hitting me with her shoulder. Flirtation was a universal language. I nodded for her to take in the length of the beach we were about to stroll, and she laughed. Her eyes widened with wonder. I think she laughed because she couldn't believe how much tropical beauty surrounded her. How endless it seemed. *Haiti, chérie. T'es trop belle, toi.* White sands, water and sky bluer than her eyes, and spritely coconut trees framing the whole thing as far as eyes could see, what's not to love? Such bounty in one place was indeed absurd, I then realized too, as if for the first time. This is my country.

Shielding her eyes from the sun, Elizabeth looked at me, as if to say, go ahead, man, say it, open up. It's cool. I hesitated and looked at her with a bashful grin that said, really, are you serious? She smiled briefly, and then took off in a sprint toward the ocean. Pulling her dress off over her head, she revealed a perfect, underwear-free ass that hovered in the air longer than seemed humanly possible before disappearing in the bosom of gentle waves. Without hesitating this time, I ran after her. The water was warm. Half the ocean filled my lungs with salt and foliage instantly, for I was a terrible swimmer. I thrashed about the water in hopes of reaching her. Instead of traveling from point A to point B, I splashed in one place. By the time I came out of the water, I felt exhausted, like I'd swum across the Atlantic and back. Elizabeth swam winningly, and, 200 meters away, she stopped and looked for me with a confused look on her face. Like, you call *that* swimming? How'd she get that far, that fast? I thought. I tried to tiptoe across the ocean toward her. She dove back in the water and disappeared. In the time it took me to slog five ginger steps, while failing to avoid drinking half the salty ocean, she emerged another 200 meters away. Oh, so you want to race, eh? I thought. I got back on land and sprinted toward her position. She waited a couple of heartbeats to gauge my speed, then she dove back in the water. Her nude, alabaster-colored skin sliced the light blue waters like a flash of lightning. After a while, I assumed I was sufficiently ahead of her. I coasted and jumped in the water and positioned myself with a victorious grin in front of where I thought she would emerge. When she tapped me on the shoulder from behind, I realized I was wrong. My eyes widened and my jaw dropped. Water flew from my hair's giant black curls. She hugged me from behind, pressing her small breasts against my naked back. Wait, wasn't I supposed to be the one trying to seduce her? Giggling, she walked out of the water to the beach and took a seat next to our stuff. Her walk, framed by a gold-orange sun setting in a smoldering ocean, was something to behold. Such self-assurance, such grace. Her legs seemed infinitely long. Now she decided to sunbathe, eyes closed, a near smile on her beautiful face. Her hair lay flat down her chest, covering the large areolas of her nipples, which made me sad. I suddenly longed to see her breasts again more than anything else in the known world.

We shouldn't do this, I said to her after I sat down.

A guy selling coconuts walked up the beach, and I waved him over.

I mean, I shouldn't do this. I don't know what I want to do with my life. I like my dad. Correction: I love my father. I love him to death. I'll probably be following his ideas on family, honor, and love until my dying day. Yet it feels wrong to have him choose you to be my wife and for you to actually be wonderful and seemingly into me before I could even visualize what kind of husband I could, or even should, be. It feels wrong that my family life could be handed to me like a gift from a department store of good genes. What about my choices, my desires, my visions of freedom? I'm barely eighteen years old!

The coconut guy sliced off the top of the coconut with a huge machete to create a perfect sipping hole in one casually savage move and handed the coconut to me. I passed it to Elizabeth. With my coconut, he performed a grander flourish in his slicing move, like a mousquetaire. I could see this impressed Elizabeth. I gave him a nice tip. He thanked me and winked. Brothers have to look out for each other, he said in creole, with a toothy grin.

Sipping on her coconut, Elizabeth looked at me with expectant eyes, like she expected me to continue my monologue. This freaked me out. She wasn't supposed to understand what I was saying. *Merde*, suppose she did? Relax, Gil, she doesn't. Keep your rich-kid blues to yourself, man.

I'm going to be a filmmaker, you know, Elizabeth said.

I had no clue what she was saying at that time, but hoped to figure it out later. I planned to improve my German quickly to keep up with her seemingly soon-to-be-excellent French.

My parents, she continued, probably believe this forced marriage will be a chore for me. To me, you're just material for my first great movies. Our relationship, as improbable as it is, a mongrel like you with an Aryan goddess like me, could be an interesting enough experiment in debasement to inspire art that could raise a fourth Reich. I do concede that you are beautiful for a mongrel. Your Prussian half did you good service. Your looks will make being with you less painful. My parents are such fucking jokes. They killed millions of people during the war. But the minute things got tough, they turned into mealymouthed beggars of the weakest, most embarrassing kind. Sometimes they make me so angry I almost think they are Jews. I can't believe I'm the only real Nazi left in our family. I'm not one of those saps who believe the Fuhrer will rise soon from the grave and rescue Germany from the defiling hands of the Allies. However, I do believe my country has a right to feel proud of its history, its victories, along with its losses. Our knees can occasionally be bent by war gone bad, but never should we kneel and apologize. We will overcome the setbacks from what people call the Second World War, and restore our glory, I'm sure of it. We did it before. We will do it again. We will win more wars. It's so amazing that we came so close to conquering the world, how could we not try again? To get there, we'll need the help of poets and artists more than tanks and armies, in the first phase anyway. Of this I am certain. Your hot and dirty little island will inspire me, and hopefully other Nazis in the Americas, like exile from Florence served that fop Dante.

Pleased with her speech, Elizabeth lay down, gazed at the big blue ocean, and smiled. Her sun-kissed self-confidence was engrossing and seductive. I went in to kiss her. She slapped me.

What the hell?

The sunset, the beach, the lapping waves, the expectant grin, then a slap? I'll be damned. A head scratcher.

Elizabeth laughed at my befuddlement, loudly and hysterically. Apparently, she never saw anything funnier than my young, confused, and sexually frustrated face. I slapped her back. She punched me in the nose. I fell on my back, clutching my face, anticipating blood. But instead, I felt a kiss on my lips. Her hands took mine down from my face. She kissed my nose. She kissed my cheeks and ear and soon sucked on my neck, with the violence of a suction cup. My legs parted. *Her* legs parted. She mounted me and kept kissing me. Our backs arched in spasms of matching passion. Her body melted into mine on the beach while kissing me with her hungry, roaming mouth, and the surprise of her overwhelming tenderness penetrated a place inside me I was unaware existed. My body sank into the sand, like a wave after crashing on the beach. Eventually, exhausted, thrillingly, I went limp between her legs, drained, satiated.

For the rest of my life, even a couple of heartbeats before my death, I would remember every single second of that first time on the beach with Elizabeth, the Nazi beauty, even though I, like most Haitian boys, had lost my virginity years before that fateful day. Somehow the moment Elizabeth kissed me aroused a virgin's mix of fear and wonder in me, and when we made love she deflowered me anew, took something precious and tender from me, something I had forgotten I possessed and somehow immediately wanted to recapture. Postcoital, I looked at this German girl lying nude next to me with a self-satisfied look on her face on my Caribbean beach and wanted to demand she return to me my innocence.

Instead, I soon married her. I didn't have time to dwell on regrets.

5

JAZZ DES JEUNES

Are you fucking kidding me?

This was my brother Jackie's daily refrain after I told him about my intention to wed Elizabeth. We would argue about it throughout the days leading to the wedding, and we were having it out right now, in my bedroom in the mansion, minutes before the wedding ceremony. He found my choices questionable, to say the least. He was my best man.

That suit is horrible too, he said.

Really?

That tie, man, it hurts my eyes it's so ugly. Come on. You don't wear a pink tie with a blue pinstripe suit. You might as well be wearing a skirt and barrettes in your hair, Gil.

All right, Jack, calm down.

Your shoes, Gil, *mon dieu. Quelle horreur!* They're killers of good taste, monuments to bad fashion, the Mona Lisa of horrors.

I get it. You just have no class, Jack. Zoot suits are all the rage in New York City.

What do you know about New York City? You dress like a country bumpkin from the Republic of Bananas.

I'm moving there next month.

You're what?

Jackie wasn't smiling his mocking grin anymore. I stole his New York City dream from him. Learn to become a great writer in Haiti, motherfucker. I'm going to the Big Apple and you're not. I'll tell Hemingway you said hello.

Look.

I took a letter from my desk and handed it to him.

You got into Columbia University? You're going to study finance? But you barely know how to count!

I don't know what to tell you, *mon frère*. Guess somebody over there decided to not underestimate me.

You're not going to like America, Jackie said, dryly, putting the letter down gently.

He seemed to have regained his composure.

You won't be able to handle its pervasive racism.

I've been handling condescending fools all my life, Jack.

You're too soft, Gilbert. You ain't built for the harsh weather and cultures abroad. See, I've been preparing for life out there all my life. I know condescending fools in ways you can't imagine.

Write to me about it. Since you're the only one in our family with an imagination.

I'm serious, Gil. Your big goofy hair and lopsided grin won't make life easy for you in New York City, like it does here, nor will it enable you to deal with life off campus. New York life is just short of barbaric. Racism, man . . .

Only one way to find out, eh, Jack? I'll be free to find out on my own, with none of y'all around to tell me what to do and think. Freedom ain't free, but it's going to be mine, all mine. I'm not even sending you postcards. Now come do your duty as my best man and help me with these cufflinks. I want to look as fresh as Gatsby.

Gatsby? What do you know about Gatsby?

I sighed.

Jackie believed he was the only person in our family who could read books and dream. He really believed that. Now that I'm about to die, I can say he was right in a way. I could read, and I did read a lot more novels and other books than most football players, but I was no writer, scholar, or philosopher. The dreams that emerged from my reading and reflection were mostly reactions to other people's dreams, especially Jackie's or Dad's, sometimes Mom's. Definite echoes of women I loved. I did things to impress, or fuck, but not because my heart was in those things. I never could give shape to my freedom. I was lost in it, you know? I would struggle all my life, traveling the world, to figure out where, and to whom, my heart belonged. I was free, as free as the stars, so free! But I yearned to be tethered too. I don't know why. As a result, I would struggle with some form of heartbreak most of my life. I guess today, seconds from my execution, sans last meal, by the way, my mistake was thinking my struggle was unique, that my nagging sense of incompletion, was mine and mine alone. Aurélie was my anchor, and I managed to underestimate that.

What about your soon-to-be wife? Jackie asked.

Who?

Elizabeth. The white girl, race man. Just when black Haitians, like black people across the world, start finding our voices to politically carve out a bigger piece of the pie, you, you go and marry the whitest woman you meet two seconds after you met. Sigh. What a useless waste of good genes you are to the black community.

She, she'll be fine, I said.

The political dimension of his argument staggered me. This was the first time I was confronted with the idea that I owed some positivity to the black half of my heritage. This mostly downtrodden community had been an afterthought for me like . . . it was for my father.

For my life up until that day, all I thought I had going for me was that I took orders well, and, like most attractive people, I was good at winning approval. I gave good theater. This day, for the first time in my young life, I learned that my life could mean something more, could be of service, that the theater that is me could give pleasure and, gasp, inspiration to the least lucky of Haiti. The idea seeped into me slowly, like good medicine.

My mother poked her head into the room, a frozen smile on her face. She wore almost no makeup. I noticed such things. Was she protesting my nuptials by paring down her beauty? I knew she didn't approve of me marrying That German Girl, as she would call her to her dying day. The accusatory stares she threw Papa over the dinner table, everywhere, really, during the days leading up to the wedding could have killed a herd of rhino. Because she beautified herself when even her most random friend visited us, her toned-down look for my wedding made me feel like I was preparing to attend a funeral. Her sadness was naked and pure, buckling my knees. Jackie promptly got up, lowered his eyes, and left the room without saying a word.

Sit, Mother said to me, pointing to my bed as she took a seat on an armchair. Outside, a couple of thick gray clouds stepped in front of the midday sun.

Did you know I was your age when I married your father? she said.

I failed to hide surprise from my face.

Yes, I was eighteen years old once, too, believe it or not.

Then Mother paused. What was to follow was meant to be serious, the theme of our conversation. The Message. It came loud and clear. Even though we moved more slowly around the world than you kids do today, she said, I do know what it's like to follow your heart, or mainly your id, not your head or your parents' heads. I know about the power of a *coup de foudre*, the lure of a foreign adventure. I know about love and hate. I definitely know about duty and pain.

I know you do, *Maman.*

I mean it.

I believe you.

She did not.

Elizabeth is a nice girl, *Maman. Je l'aime bien.* She has a tough air about her. She seems capable of handling herself and any problems life will throw our way. Our love is not obvious, but it's not bad.

Tchippp!!!

Mother sucked her teeth. The Caribbean woman's universal sign of skepticism and disgust.

You know I love you more than my own flesh and blood, but you did inherit some of your father's bullshitter tendencies. Be careful. I doubt this Nazi girl will take as much shit from you as I took from your father. You might end up in a gas chamber if you sleep around on her.

Maman!

Sorry. I couldn't resist that joke. *Venez, mon fils. Que dieu te protége.*

Mother hugged me so hard I struggled to breath.

Mon dieu, you grew up too fast, she said, adding, with a whisper, I'll always be here for you.

. . .

The wedding unfolded like a bright, fantastic dream. Day-Glo colors everywhere. Lots of pinks, yellows, greens, reds, whites, and oranges, and a blazing blue sky that was so blue, so pretty, so unique to Haiti's sky and ocean, it seemed like the preeminent color of heaven. It must be. Our various servants lined the halls of the house as I walked through the hallway leading to the vast living room, with its sofas and pillows and wicker chairs, before walking outside into our garden. The sun perked up high and hot. The day was insanely humid. The guests all turned around from facing the altar to watch me walk down the aisle. I felt ridiculously young in the moment, like a child in a grown man's suit. My outfit felt stupid. I hated when Jackie was proven right. I trudged toward the altar and the waiting priest. Remembering this was supposed to be a festive occasion, I fixed my posture, turned on a smile, and started waving at familiar faces in the crowd. Pope mode. They were mostly parents of my friends from school, business partners of my father's. In front, I saw Elizabeth's mother sitting next to mine. She wore a fretful expression and frozen smile.

Papa. He gave me the I'm-proud-of-you nod and smile and a cheesy thumbs-up. I was happy to see him happy. What could go wrong from that? This move will turn out okay if Papa thinks it will, I told myself. I was ridiculously young and not a little naïve about life and love, especially love. I took my place next to the priest, Monsignor Tilou, the most soft-spoken Haitian in history. I wished I hadn't worn a pink tie.

We watched Elizabeth walk down the aisle with her father. She looked defiant. He looked defeated. People didn't know what to make of them. *Ça va?* she said upon reaching me. Why did she ask me if I was okay? In French! Why was everyone asking me that in one way or the other? Did I look scared or worried or something? I suppose I did. She had become fluent in French within weeks of her arrival in Haiti. Her facility with languages was impressive, and the German accent was a thrilling turn-on during sex. I didn't know what the fuck I was doing, but watching this beautiful slender bit of Teutonic steel walk toward me, willingly, as if out of a Renaissance painting, in the burning Caribbean afternoon, convinced me that I would somehow find a way to make whatever the future held for us work. I hadn't worked a day in my life, or managed anything other than my appetites, but there I was, believing I could construct a family and life with and for a woman I'd just met. Promising to build a family with a girl who seems as little a woman as I was barely a man did not ruin me, though. The forces that would ruin me were more ancient than that. Freedom is not as free as I yearned. It's quite expensive.

I do, I said, after Monsignor Tilou asked if I promised to have and to hold Elizabeth as my wife and cherish her till death do us part. The air smelled fragrant, luxurious, breezy, and slightly pungent, tinged with oud. A lot of our guests wore expensive perfumes. Fragrances from Italy, France, Morocco filled the air. Birds burst out in song, as if someone had opened a balcony door of a house situated in the middle of a zoo.

I glanced at the crowd, and that's when I saw her, a new woman. *Une bombe.* She immediately reduced my wedding vows to lies. Partly, for I intended to honor my vows, but my heart was instantly hers, irrevocably so. She was curvy and bubbly, and her face was luminous in repose, smiling with eyes that were bright enough to make the sun jealous, and yet those eyes were also knowing, she knew me, was bemused by me, and when we locked eyes, there begat an us, and we were solid, we belonged to each other, she would protect me, I felt the stirring of a new feeling, hard like a muscle, it was devotion, yes, she inspired me to be devoted to her in a way no one could, selflessness, what was that? Me? Cherishing is so warm a feeling, tenderness and caring combined, and that would be me, that would be me with this woman, clearly my age, clearly smarter than me, yet I felt I would find within me the depth, the resources, and . . . courage? to put her happiness ahead of mine, her safety and health and happiness became of paramount importance to me for some reason, like no one else's, not even my mother's, had before her. What was this, this instinct? Overpowering, it felt greater than my own survival instinct, it was the best feeling I ever felt in my life, and it was a desire with the architecture of duty, to protect and please a woman unconditionally. It was also an honor, which created a feeling of elation inside me, an honor and a passion, yes, passion, for I also wanted to make love to this woman and also shield this woman from the worst of the world, her demons, others' demons, mine. Especially my demons, for they were many, and I struggled to shed and bury them.

Who is she? This incandescent woman. *Pétillante mais encore plus.* So much more. She triggered so many new colors and shades of love inside me, this love felt grand and rare and heavenly, a love of loves, we would become lovers who love like they have always loved each other, like their love is the most obvious thing in the known world, *une évidence*, and this love for this woman and from this woman who looks admittedly like a girl, a thick and juicy and bright-eyed girl but a girl nonetheless, with a glorious crown of big curly hair threatening to lift her up into the sky if the wind blew hard enough, this love, our love, for I could see reciprocity in her eyes, felt it in my bones and intestines, like she had existed inside me with affection all my life, before we were even born, since before Christ, the time before the first dawn in the world, the first divine pregnancy. I didn't panic or fluster in the face of this realization and its blinding light, the halo of the bond that bound us, *c'était tellement évident, et une valeur sûre, la plus chère et tendre de ma vie*, and this sultry young woman had style. She wore a pink dress, and it was very short, showing off her long, shiny legs in their flagrant shapeliness. Her toes were painted white and the arch of her foot in her high heels instantly gave me a foot fetish I never knew I had, and that I could not imagine living without. She was beautiful and also cute, impish yet also majestic. But her style suggested effort and thoroughness. She was young and had made an effort to appear as sophisticated as a wedding at the home of one of the wealthiest families in Haiti required. She was not a person from our community, but that didn't matter for I was hers, and she was Haitian, one of us in the most essential way, and this I could tell from her slightly combative bearing, and again, that knowingness in her eyes, which came off as cocky, like the best of us, especially our women, always, but then, also, came my realization of the first hurdle for this love affair born of eye contact, a glance of eternal proportions, that the end of my wedding ceremony also begat the end of my marriage. The hurdle was not my new wife, for she was a matter of familial duty, a business transaction as old as the words *family* and *fortune*, as my mother suggested, but ours was a heaven-sent union, I'd gone to mass enough when God manifested himself in me, and He told me the right thing for me to do, the path to take at a fork in the road, and, today, by some miracle, all roads led to her.

The problem was her date, not mine. The man standing next to her with a boyfriend's warmth was my brother. Jackie was clapping, applauding my nuptials cheerfully, oblivious to the robbery my heart just committed and yearned to see through. The entire gathering was giving me and Elizabeth a standing ovation after the priest pronounced us man and wife. Elizabeth was taking in the applause and drinking the attention with her customary haughtiness. Her chutzpah was adorable, well-calibrated to challenge and earn the respect of damning Haitian eyes. There was an elegance to the arrogant Teuton that softened her allure to that of a young princess. She surveyed her subjects from a thatched pedestal. Haitians don't take kindly to people with royalty complexes, and we're particularly allergic to grandiose white folks, but Elizabeth was inoffensive. Trying too hard, she possessed too slight a presence in this ancient, multifaceted, weathered, and tumultuous community to be taken too seriously. What's a Nazi when you've already fought Christopher Columbus, Napoleon, and the troops of Woodrow fucking Wilson?

Ce ne sera pas facile, I thought. *Mais rien n'est facile pour nous.*

All relationships come with asterisks. Life is an asterisk, I would soon learn.

You may now kiss the bride, Monsignor Tilou said.

My eyes were fixed on the pretty little caramel woman standing next to Jackie and applauding with hands sheathed in white gloves. Her eyes turned to Elizabeth to remind me of the business at hand.

Elizabeth turned my face toward her and kissed me hard, throwing her whole body into mine and wrapping her arms tightly around my neck. Her small waist felt nice in my beefy hands, I went with the moment, cupping her with one arm, leaning into her, she took the cue and kicked a leg up. My other arm shot up for dramatic effect. A picture-perfect moment for a pretty young couple on a typically perfect afternoon in Haiti, a gorgeous, traumatized land where few pretty things and people stayed or stayed that way too long. Heroes in a tragedy. Or tragic figures playing at successful rebels? Pictures are not X-rays of the hearts of men and women.

We walked down the aisle under a shower of flowers and cheers. Older folks often look a bit marveled when young people marry, like, wow, that kind of love still exists? The fools! Younger folks thought we were nuts too, but weddings are, above all, great parties, filled with romantic possibilities of the highest order, so my friends were having a blast.

I found them standing under a shower of pink and white balloons, holding bottles of champagne up high to greet me. My wiry main man Jeremy Kahn held two bottles of champagne aloft. Salute! said Cedric Fidele, *un métisse Suisse et bon vivant extraordinaire.* Peter Druian, the wisest-looking eighteen-year-old in the world, cradled a bottle of champagne like the baby he thought I was doomed to have next. Studly Nick Chiles, our gifted goalkeeper, the most reliable human in the history of man, took a huge chug of his bottle of champagne, shook up the bottle then sprayed the shit out of me and the whole crew in celebration, of course, miming all the sex I was going to have with my new wife. Philippe Cayol, impish and irrepressible as ever, held a bottle of champagne with one hand while dancing with his girlfriend Hélène, never losing a drop of his bubbly or breaking a sweat.

You did it, Jackie said. You crazy bastard. Congratulations!

I was staring in his girlfriend's eyes and deeply in love. His voice came from far, far away. Her eyes were dark brown and deep and wondrous, two infinity pools of *douceur* and light. They held my eyes without blinking. We understood each other, in our silent language, like we had already spoken of our love, meeting in a public place, the importance of discretion from others despite the fire of our desires, the ancient *pas de deux* of forbidden love. Our bond was implacable when seen up close. I imagine her and I fooling around in the deserts of Timbuktu back when Europe was in the throes of its Middle Ages and Africa was Eden, unspoiled and royally fun. I didn't even know her name, and it didn't even matter. Maybe I didn't know it back when we were children in the Sahel six hundred years ago either. Maybe I don't need to know it. She's my other half. That is all. The world, hell, the universe, in its infinity, was going to try to come between us. Let it try.

Congratulations, she said.

Merci, I said.

Where are my manners? Jackie said. Gilbert, meet Aurélie, my fiancée. Aurélie, *voici mon petit frère*, Gilbert.

Enchanté, I said.

I held her hand. Her gaze was mine and mine was hers. You could hear our hearts beat as one.

Our eyes never left each other's even as the party around us grew louder and raged outrageously. We smiled knowing smiles at each other. I held her hand far, far longer than was appropriate, and my other hand took hers too, and when some dancer bumped me into her, I thought I heard the priest repeat, you may now kiss the bride.

6

AIMÉ OU AIMÉ

This boy needs saving, Aurélie thought, staring up at the tall boy with the most sensual face she'd ever seen in her life. *Mon dieu, que me faites Vous la? Ce garçon est un désastre. Il vient de se marié. Et il n'arrête pas de me dévorer avec ces yeux! La sueur de la bénédiction de son mariage baigne son front. Et nous faisons l'amour avec nos yeux devant tout le monde! C'est irrésistible ce que je ressens pour cet homme en ce moment.* Wait, what, what's he doing? He's taken both my hands with his, and, and, he's pulling me to the dance floor? But I'm your brother's date, she said, in the weakest protest.

That sounds like an invitation, Aurélie, Gilbert said, with a grin.

Ironically, the band for the party was Jazz des Jeunes. The bandleader, in a twist of awful wit, had the band play their hit dirge, "Trahison," when he saw the groom smoothly start dancing with a beautiful woman, not his wife. The inappropriate couple danced and danced, gracefully, a sizzling tango. Soon, they levitated, lifting off the dance floor, imperceptibly at first, but inexorably, the young lady in the pink dress and the young man in the zoot suit were soon waltzing above the crowd. People looked up admiringly at the bottom of their shoes. They formed an adorable and stylish couple, and they danced so well to the slow, sexy, and mournful song, like love after the novelty wears off and the good groove starts. Serenity. Aurélie and Gilbert were the picture of sensual synchronicity. If two young dancers hadn't floated above a dance floor in Haiti before this night, it was about time a couple did. The '40s had been good to Haiti. No occupiers, no dictators, democracy, security, rule of law, all Haitian enforced, this had people feeling modern, in step with the world. American in the best sense of the word in their optimism.

A long skinny hand reached up and tugged at Gilbert's ankle and pulled them back down to earth. It was Gil's mother. She sized up Aurélie, and, after a pause for dramatic effect, she indicated her approval. She also gave Gilbert that be careful look, a mother's reflex.

Viens, mon chéri, I have someone I want you to meet, she said.

Gilbert and his mother walked across the ballroom and the silky chaos of dancers, gyrating people who were now dancing on the walls and even on the ceilings. The levitation dance Aurélie and Gilbert invented caught on. Gil made sure to give Aurélie a reassuring, I'll be right back look, which he hadn't given his wife. His wife. He hadn't thought about her for a while, so he straightened his posture. Husband mode. It came to him naturally. You represent a team when you're married. You had to look like you had a spine now.

Aimé, Aimé.

Mom was tapping the shoulder of a short rotund man with glasses and a face that dazzled with intelligence. He was accompanied by a tall pale woman with the vigilant eyes of a hawk. He had a group of brothers in stitches with jokes and stories. All the guys had black wives. For some reason I began noting such things.

Gilbert, meet Aimé Césaire, the great writer from Martinique. He is visiting Haiti for a literary conference on *la négritude* and the untapped power of the black imagination, and he graciously attended your wedding.

Aimé, voici Gilbert, mon seul et unique fils.

Mes felicitations, Gilbert, the great man said. Your wedding is one of the most joyous weddings I've ever attended. Look at all these young people dancing on the ceilings! Your love is truly inspiring.

Thank you, sir, Gil said, but um, actually, that dance was created by another woman.

Already? *Mon dieu*, you Haitians move fast, don't you?

Everyone laughed.

Aimé took me by an elbow.

Allons, he said, let's take a walk.

We walked through a throng of well-wishers and dancers. They gave me high-fives while dancing on walls or upside down from the ceiling. Outside, beyond a large terrace, the lights of Port-au-Prince twinkled in the heavens and at our feet. I thought of Aurélie and wanted to show her the beauty of the sparkling stars from my home.

Comment vas tu, jeune homme?

A bit too excited, I think.

I would say so.

What?

I saw you fall in love with your brother's girlfriend during your wedding.

What?! No, sir, you're mistaken.

We all did, son. Well, those of us who've been in your

predicament immediately recognized it. You're fucked, my young friend.

I am, aren't I?

Yes, son, you are. But that's okay.

Really?

Yes, you're going to suffer. A great deal. But you will become a wiser man from such an experience. If it doesn't kill you, of course.

Césaire smiled.

I smiled, crestfallen. Pain was coming. The price of great love is a disproportionate number of nightmares. I can feel it. Even so, the idea of dying for Aurélie appealed to me for some reason.

Unexpected, inappropriate love is brutal, Césaire said, but it's a part of life. It's the best and worst moment of every life. You can't control it. Love is an act of God. A miracle we can't anticipate or control, though it blows our minds each and every time with its grandeur and hint of doom. That's why we often compare it to natural disasters like lightning strikes or hurricanes, or tornados and tsunamis. Love happens without warning, abruptly, and when it's true, it is always breathtaking. That's why love simultaneously makes us yearn for respite, soothing sex, caresses and flowers, all that is gentle in the world. To appease us. Calm our palpitating hearts. I tell you, kid, love is a terrible thing. A terrible, terrible thing.

He glances nervously at his tall lady in the distance. She lurked in the shadows, surrounded by the thickets of ivy that draped the mansion's walls. Her hawk eyes beaming red.

Anyway, my boy, didn't mean to scare you anymore than you already are.

He must have noticed that my hair was standing up

straight, almost a mile high in the sky. I was wide-eyed and very scared.

He smiled a sad smile.

I do have one very important piece of advice for you, Gilbert, he said.

I was all ears.

Always treat the black woman you love honorably. If you love . . .

Aurélie.

. . . Aurélie, like you feel you love her right now, you must avoid taking her as your mistress. In my country, Martinique, there's an old tradition of black men marrying the white woman for practical reasons and keeping the black woman we actually love as our mistress. It's a cruel legacy of colonialism. And, like all legacies of colonialism, it must end. *Mon jeune ami*, you have to do better than the rest of us. Haiti is the birthplace of *la négritude*. You are the future of Haiti. You have to set a good example for your people, our people, the blackest people on earth, literally and figuratively. Haiti already set the greatest example for black love in history, with its incredible revolution against enslavement. Whether Haitians accept the responsibility or not, for better and for worse, the rest of us look to Haitians to keep doing better than we can under the shadow of colonialism. The black woman should never enter your life *par la petite porte*, Gilbert. You must treat her like the greatest thing to happen to you. To the world. Which she is.

Yes, she is, I said, under my breath, staring at the lights of the city shining in the distance. I felt that volcanic surge of emotions and thoughts of Aurélie burn inside me.

There's a new era coming, where black is beautiful, Césaire continued, where black love will set the standard of beauty for everyone. Haiti has a new opportunity to set the example. The unity of the black man and the black woman should rise above the colonial garbage of our history that tries to dictate our present.

Hell, yes.

You're young and privileged. I counted three presidents of Haiti at your wedding, the best writers and painters too. I am genuinely impressed. How many kids' weddings attract such illustrious guests?! Everyone likes you and your parents. You represent Haiti's future. Its best and brightest. Let Haiti's future be one where black men treat black women as their cherished beloved, not hidden pleasures, or distant kissing cousins.

With that, the old man placed a hand on my shoulder and gave me one last friendly smile.

I smiled back. His message was a poignant one. I nodded my appreciation.

He ambled toward his lady in waiting, and I watched them disappear into the party with people dancing on walls. A *rara* was playing. Carnival music tipped with sinister drums and flutes evoking nocturnal, dirty dancing ancestors. Below me, the lights of Port-au-Prince seemed to be dancing to the music too. Everyone was having fun in Haiti this night. Except me. I felt tears well up in my eyes. Aurélie should have been the woman who became my wife on that stage today. *Mon dieu*, if only I'd met her before I met Elizabeth! Now I can't be with the woman I loved. This realization was wounding but had to have a solution somewhere, I thought in mounting panic. I couldn't see it in the big black sky above me. The answers were hidden behind the stars. They had to find me someday. They had to.

Then I smelled a woman's perfume. Bergamot. Before I

could turn around, she wrapped her arms around me and held me tight. I felt one of my ribs crack. She buried her head against my back. I closed my eyes and inhaled deeply, savoring the moment. Which woman was this? Please, God, I pray it's my wife.

I'm tired, she said.

It was Aurélie!

Take me home, she said. Your brother's too drunk to drive.

7

CITÉ SOLEIL KISSES

Sometimes you must say no to a beautiful woman's invitation. This was probably one of those times. In fact, this certainly was one of those times. But I was not wise the night I met Aurélie Fabienne Picard. Nor did I want to be.

We walked, no, floated through the party toward the big front door. We felt too high on each other to bother touching the ground. I saw Jackie was indeed passed out at a piano, drooling into a bottle of champagne. I waved at him, as if I was telling him I was going to do him a favor now and take his girlfriend home. The most disingenuous wave in history. Aurélie looked at him sweetly, like she was pleased he was sleeping blissfully. The woman did not possess a single shred of doubt in the rightness of us despite the outrageous circumstances, and her confidence was contagious. The Germans were nowhere to be seen. Early bedtime for mass murderers? Elizabeth was still partying though. In the middle of a circle of new friends, she was learning to do Josephine Baker moves to many ooooohs and aaaaaahs and seemingly having a very good time, as she deserved. Lose your European ways, girl, Haiti got you. It was my turn to offer a distant sweet smile. Elizabeth was going to be fine with or without me. I thought Elizabeth was too caught up in the rapture of dancing to the roaring drums of Ti Roro and Jazz des Jeunes to notice my betrayal, but she did. She didn't pause long enough for the tears welling in her eyes to merge with the sweat pouring down her face. She didn't run after me either. Why not? I don't know. She did grow to hate me ferociously, leading to my imprisonment and execution. So, there's that.

My father was dancing upside down in a dark corner of the ceiling with a bountiful woman who seemed to have swallowed him whole with her buxom body. His eyes were closed, and his face had that look of agony and ecstasy that only a good, slow dance in a Caribbean party could generate. The dances are often so sensual, they can feel like sex itself. Even better. They are akin to a prelude to sex that can feel like a climax, a continuous one. If you're lucky enough one night to find yourself on a dance floor captured by traditional music with the right person on a French Caribbean island, you can live out an entire love affair dancing forehead to forehead, slowly, grindingly, with a suite of minimalist moves, to keep time, to subtly remind observers that caressing and body-merging while accompanied by plaintive singing and booming drums is a sensual tradition as old and black and luminous as our souls. That dance will feel like the greatest, most vital moment of your entire life and the end will feel like a death, *un petit mort.*

My pinkie reached for Aurélie's, discreetly. She took it and her eyes lit up.

Maman nous regardait. I could sense it. She was at a table on my right with a dozen serious celebrities, including the current and recent presidents of Haiti, a few senators, the writers Jacques Roumain, Marie Vieux-Chauvet, and Stephen Alexis, and our visiting luminaries from Martinique: Aimé Césaire, the activist Sarita Smith Fanfant and her husband, the legendary drummer Jean-Philippe, Sandrine Désiré the fiery politician, the doting sisters Dany and Edith Bruere-Dawson, the academics Philippe Boniface and Nathaly Psyché, and Valerie Wolnerman, the stunning Olympian. You gotta love people from Martinique. They are the most beautiful multicultural black people you'll ever meet, and they behaved as if such a state of grace was the most natural thing in the world. They were thoroughly Parisian in language and demeanor, but they spoke with flourishes of creole that charmed to no end, and when the music hit, they danced and drank rum as if wasting a beat and a drop were crimes. I would later learn they were the last lovely and friendly part of the French empire, shining examples of the best *metissage* of European wealth and Afro-Caribbean pride in the world. Mother's table had so many bold thinkers and revolutionary spirits it looked like a Bois Caiman meeting for the mid-twentieth century. Mom looked at me with regal amusement. She gave our butler a nod. He tossed me car keys. Clearly, black love, like mine with Aurélie, was a revolutionary act she would sponsor. The odds were against us, but the odds are always against black love, aren't they? Maybe that's why Haitians love so damn hard when we love. Nothing good lasts too long with us.

Soon, Aurélie and I were easing out of the compound and heading west toward centre-ville. In front of the massive white walls of the Oasis Hotel, before going into la Route de Bourdon, I take a long loving look at this woman who had captivated me to the point of hijacking my wedding night. The big curly hair, the succulent deep brown and flawless skin, the plunging neckline that led to the center of the multiverse, the slender fingers, the bright pink fingernails. *Tout a croquer!* We drive past Impasse Pierre-Louis, home to my favorite cousins, who I last saw dancing on the ceilings around the mansion with the sassiest women at the party. Looking at Aurélie, I can't believe my luck. It couldn't last long, could it? Except Aurélie and I felt so natural together that being together felt easy, effortless, like luck had nothing at all to do with it. We cruised toward the National Palace, home to the president now partying at my crib, sat across from Champs de Mars, emerging from the dark in the burnt oranges of dawn. Imposing, powerful. A surge of patriotic pride fired through my heart, then panic. You can't have love without its twin, deathly fear of losing it, can you? I glanced furtively at my love. I opened my palm, silently imploring her to take it and please hold me and hold on to us. She did. She did! We clasped hands and stared straight ahead at Port-au-Prince undulating before us like the future, a dream of happiness destined to come true.

What's wrong?

Nothing, I said, I just want to feel like we're on a date and coming out of the movies. What's your favorite movie?

Anything with Sidney Poitier.

Mine too!

Then we reached Pont Rouge, the place where Jean-Jacques Dessalines, Haiti's first president, was assassinated. Dismembered actually. Messy, so messy. Come to think of it, Pont Rouge is close to Fort Dimanche, where I stand right now, many years later, awaiting my own execution. On that fateful night, the road to Cité Soleil, the ghetto where Aurélie lived, was treacherous and forbidden to me and all sensible folks for safety reasons. It was a rough neighborhood, and not an ideal place for me to be driving with a beautiful neighborhood girl in the middle of the night in a red Mercedes-Benz convertible.

I think we're going to be fine together, I said.

Aurélie leaned her head against my shoulder and purred like a cat. It was the wee hours of the morning. Soft and cool and ever so mournful, like a Sinatra song. I drove with practiced calm. Aurélie could tell my exotic car wasn't meant to go slow. It yearned to unleash its roar. A bit like its owner, she thought wickedly. It wasn't safe to drive slow in Port-au-Prince in the dark. But she liked that I wanted to drive real slow. He wanted to be with me, she told herself, and he wanted to make sure every second together was stretched out and enjoyed to the max. I appreciated that, and every other second, I thought this boy needs me to save him from the life he was raised to have, which, despite its glamour, has some dramatic differences with the life he craved deeply, the life that would be good for him. How did Aurélie know all this only a few hours after meeting Gil? The heart knows.

I think we'll be fine too, she said, if you don't get us killed tonight.

What do you mean?

You drive like my great-grandmother.

Next thing she knew, the Benz leapt in the air like a toro and peeled through the streets. At Pont Rouge, the car slowed down a little, as if it wanted to pay respect to his heroes Jean-Jacques Dessalines and Toussaint Louverture, the Beninois who led Haiti's successful revolt against France.

Okay, okay, tiger, calm down, Aurélie said. You proved your point. I'm going to start law school next week when you go to New York City. You don't want the scholarship I got to go to waste.

Really? So, you're as smart as you are pretty. What kind of lawyer do you want to be? Are you going to be able to keep me from going to hell?

Why do you think you're going to hell, Gil?

I punched my ticket to hell tonight, didn't I? I'm two for ten in violating the Ten Commandments. I worship your beauty and its effects on me more than I do God, and I'm coveting my brother's wife. While married to another woman, I should add.

Thanks for the compliment, but I'm not Jack's wife.

I'm violating a third commandment too, come to think of it. The one about not killing my fellow man. Jack's life is hard enough. I should not have stolen his girlfriend too. It's going to kill him.

Boy, you don't know nothing about nothing, do you? Jack's going to become a priest!

In shock, Gil drove the car onto a sidewalk on Boulevard Jean-Jacques Dessalines, startling a sleeping bum.

That's how we met. Catechism.

If you tell me you're going to become a nun, Gil screamed, I'm going to drive us straight into the ocean!

Hahahahahahaha, no, silly, but I'm a practicing Catholic, Aurélie said. I find nourishment in the faith's rituals, and I love to stay on God's good side. I like to help the monks and nuns tend to the poor at the chaplaincy in Carrefour when I have free time. There's a lot of poor people to help.

We pull into Cité Soleil. There's the obligatory burning drum barrel to greet us. Five of them. I can feel their heat singe my curly hair as I drive around them. Menacing men idle on the streets. It's cliché to call a man in Cité Soleil menacing, but these niggas are scary as fuck. What the hell are they doing on the streets during these hours instead of in bed or at a party with their ladies? You can only see their teeth in the darkness. A few recognize Aurélie. My pulse calms a little. I see the flash of silver of machetes being sheathed.

Her house was nice, the nicest on the block, probably the nicest in Cité Soleil. The first time in his life the words *nice* and *Cité Soleil* were used in the same sentence.

Dit donc, he said, *ta vie n'est pas mal, la catho.* She shrugged.

They kissed.

So passionately that their teeth smashed before their tongues tickled and swabbed their entire faces.

Without fuss, she straddled him. The car seat reclined. They moaned and moaned, oh, they moaned.

Stray dogs howled. Other dogs started barking. Cats panicked and sprinted away. Gangsters paused from sharpening their machetes and nodded in appreciation of the sounds of love booming through the night sky. A light turned on in the kitchen of Aurélie's house. Parents wondering who the fuck was making that noise.

She screamed.

Aurélie! he screamed.

She returned to her seat, panting.

Gil looked over at her, incredulous, dazed, and happy.

Please wait for me, my Penelope, he says.

I will, my Odysseus.

I will.

8

HARLEM BLUES

Life in New York City was crushingly boring my first months there. Gloomy. Perpetually gloaming skies. Constant agitation trapped in a spiderweb of sadness and hurry for too-fleeting good times. The buildings were indeed very tall. The skies were sometimes blindingly blue and sunny the September I started my studies, but they became oppressively gray and windy and cold every month after that. The view of the gleaming city from the back of the taxi crossing the 59th Street bridge the morning I landed was spectacular. The metallic grid that held the bridge gave the onrushing big city a combo of frenzy and cool that would amaze me forever. But my enthusiasm deflated a bit when I discovered I lived in a fifth-floor walk-up apartment in a building with no elevator. The stairwell was too narrow for my broad shoulders. I had to learn to make myself smaller somehow. And when the incandescent sun of September morphed into the bite of October, I discovered some of my classmates' favorite pastime was to try to make me feel smaller too.

Where are you from?

What are you?

These kids were mostly my age and lily white, but hard. Many had fought in the war, but even those who didn't had a hard edge about them. The professors did too. Maybe I was merely bruised by my first contacts with adulthood and the demands of professionalism in a giant, crowded new school and country and a city so cold and efficient it felt like it arrived from a mean future. Maybe I was merely lonely. My roommate hadn't arrived yet. I'd sit in the armchair in my living room and stare forlornly at the sofa and imagine conversations I'd love to have after a long day of classes, which included some English classes. Those were not bad. They had the benefit of including people with brown faces like mine, and they looked as lost and overwhelmed by the rigors of life in a vast, fast new country as I was. I tried to strike up conversations with them after class but failed to connect. The walks home alone were long. I avoided crossing through campus in Morningside Heights. I didn't want to run into classmates. I didn't want to hear the questions of what I was. Are you a spic? You can't be a nigger. Niggers don't speak French. You an Indian? What's Haiti? How do you pronounce that?

I sometimes worried I would forget how to speak, for I spoke so little. I had to look at my reflection in the windows of stores on Broadway to remind myself what I looked like, since I didn't have many chances to see my reflection in the eyes of others. And I didn't own a mirror at home. Looking back at that time, I was lonely, the common affliction of immigrants, the underbelly of international adventure, when you feel like no one knows how to pronounce your name and they don't care to. I didn't have money issues. I didn't have trouble meeting people. But I had trouble feeling understood and appreciated. Does anyone ever get understood in the course of their entire lives? Probably not. But when you don't speak the same language with the right swagger, and you don't look like the majority of people in a country, you can feel nonexistent, invisible, and the road to acceptance doesn't come with a map. Inclusion abroad is never as facile as it is back home. Inclusion can happen, though. Love happens. But loneliness is your daily bread to start, inevitably. I was too embarrassed to get my mouth to form the word *lonely*. It's not a word or condition that Haitians allow to happen in Haiti. In the entire Caribbean, we don't allow loneliness to take root. Oh, I'm sure it attempts to. You can *choose* to be alone, but loneliness? Nope. At the merest hint of loneliness, you merely leave your room or your house and go down the street and talk to the first stranger you meet. In markets, people actively make eye contact. You could talk to that woman selling the fruit you don't even know or even like for an hour, and it's okay. She might stop by your house for dinner on her way home later or another day. And that's okay too. Food is often shared. Doors are *always* open. To acquaintances, randoms, friends of friends, cousins, within reason, of course. Shiftiness is common too and gotta be avoided. Though sometimes you can't help letting a shady person in your life, because well, sneaky people are sometimes very entertaining.

I would later learn there were neighborhoods in New York City that operated like Port-au-Prince. Quarters where immigrants lived like we did in our tropical communities. They were in Queens, Brooklyn, the Bronx, but I didn't know those things in the autumn of '49. I knew Morningside Heights and the Columbia University campus, and my off-putting classmates, distant professors, and kind shopkeepers and my ghosting roommate.

I was becoming a regular at mass at St. John the Divine, the cathedral across the street from my apartment, on 110th and Amsterdam. Its spires cast a shadow that cut through my living room, which I discovered one stormy night after a flash of lightning introduced me to its gothic girth outside my window. I began going to mass there on Sundays. I was raised Catholic, but my parents didn't go to mass or encourage me to go to mass. I'd spend Sunday mornings reading, feeling through a football injury, waiting for the oppressive morning heat of Port-au-Prince to cool off before going to meet the fellas for a kick-about late in the afternoon. But meeting Aurélie inspired me to return to God. The schizophrenia of loving her and becoming a husband to Elizabeth was driving me nuts. Who else but God could help me tackle the mysteries of those two types of love warring inside me?

During my last weeks in Haiti, I'd spend my mornings at home most days making love to Elizabeth. Our parents wanted us to have a baby as soon as possible. We liked to make love. A win-win. Sometimes I was tired of their demands and wanted to tell all of them to go fuck themselves and have the baby without me, but the duty of producing an heir was part of my deal with my father. He would remind me of our deal whenever he could.

You made some free kicks today, son? he'd ask. Other times, he'd say, *Doit au but, mon garçon.*

On weekday afternoons, during the hours when I'd normally be playing football, I'd make my way to the chaplaincy in Carrefour to spend time with Aurélie. Jackie would be there too. The first time we saw each other doing charity work at the chaplaincy wasn't even awkward.

Saint Gil in the house!

We shook hands and hugged.

Wearing his white collar and priest's robe in the chaplaincy, near a church, Jackie was different, yet the same. He was the same reliably affectionate brother. But gone was the timid boy I grew up with on our compound. He had confidence, a gentle swagger. He was even kind to me, the interloper in his place of work, his community of worship and charity.

Aurélie told me you were coming.

You didn't believe her, did you?

God works in mysterious ways, Gil.

Answer the question, Jack.

Did I believe that your self-interest coincided with your romantic interests and doing God's work? Sure. What you're really asking is do I hold that against you? Nope. Look at the poor beggars around us, Gil. There are millions of people like this in Haiti. Millions. They don't care where your inspiration for charity work comes from. Not one bit. Deliver them a little peace. I'll be happy. They'll be happy. God will be happy.

Yes, we'd give food, water, and a compassionate ear to the poor. Sometimes we'd go to mass together in the evenings, Aurélie, Jackie, and I. I enjoyed giving my time to charity. I started getting my dad to donate more and more stuff for the church to give away. Sure, he said. He didn't care. That was great. I gave away enough money to build a new orphanage, and I equipped it with a store, a mess hall. It was the right thing to do. Summer went by too fast. I was leaving soon, and I started to feel bad about that. Why leave Haiti when I was just getting the hang of being a good citizen? Why leave Aurélie when seeing her every day gave me the main reason to get out of bed in the morning? I just wanted to be near her and smell her and discreetly touch her. I hoped sharing the practice of our faith would boost the righteousness of our love, so it could temper the flagrant adultery of it all and become something good and special I could carry with me abroad, pray that our faith in God, like our love, would protect me from temptation and bad luck and keep her loyal to me when she shouldn't be in the tough years ahead. That habit of going to church and praying, not just for us, but for strangers, everyone, even non-Haitians, soon made its way inside my veins and began to pacify my roiling heart and fearful spirits a little, temporarily, for what was a Catholic mass but an opportunity to share our terrors and wishes with God and convince ourselves that all our problems would disappear an hour later?

In New York City, at St. John the Divine, I also prayed every Wednesday and Sunday for relief from the yawning emptiness I felt without Aurélie and Jackie by my side. My reward for attending mass was a surprise and amazing jolt of joy at the end when Father Campi had us wish peace to our fellow congregants. Sometimes they smiled and made vigorous eye contact with me. Other times, people made a token gesture, a wan wave. Either way, I felt seen! This feeling generated a great sense of belonging that eluded me outside the church pews. The crowded city where people avoided eye contact was wearying. The greetings of a handful of parishioners warmed me up and made me feel part of something greater than myself, a hopeful community. Made me aware of things, qualities, I possessed and had to share, and this eased the longing for the things and people I couldn't possess back in Haiti.

Chère Aurélie,

These past three months were the worst three months of my life. I didn't see you once. I didn't smell you or touch you or hear your voice. Oh, I love your voice. You sound more like a lawyer every day. You sounded like a lawyer before you went to law school too. So precise and clear in your thinking.

I'm a man of action, not words. But my life is boring these days. Not a lot of action. Just classes and homework. I miss Haiti so much I don't want to make friends in America. Not yet anyway. I don't want to get swept up in new social circles. You know me, I get swept up a bit too easily.

So I live like a hermit, more like a monk. I won't even masturbate. I'm saving all I am for you. I wish we had the technology to talk by video. I wish you could send me pictures instantly of your mood and outfit of the day. I wish I could see your hands, fingers. God knows I wish I could see your dimples. You're cute even in repose, even when you're mad at me, and even when confronted by a disagreeable-smelling beggar. You were extremely cute, a saucy ball of chocolate beauty, the night we met. Best night of my life.

It was not the most ideal circumstances. But I've made peace with that, chérie. You are my life. The rest is a job, work for my father. Our relationship is sacred. The rest, pffft, temporary. Business.

College studies are part of a business trip. New York City? Just another business environment. No more, no less. You may not hear from me often. You won't see me for a while. But keep things tight for me, okay? I'm tethered to you across all these miles and borders and the Caribbean ocean by a million, zillion, invisible chains. Wherever you are, and wherever I am, you are my home, my one and only love.

Yours forever,
Gil

One Wednesday night, after church, I bounded up the stairs home, buoyed by my growing faith's injections of practical applications of hope. I was almost eager for the night of cheap pizza and soda and homework awaiting me, but one particular night, when I reached my floor I was stopped in my tracks by a bolt of white-hot fear. I saw the scariest thing you can see in New York City: your apartment door open. After suppressing a scream for help, I leaned against the wall, so I couldn't be seen from the inside. I tiptoed toward the door, straining to hear what was going on inside.

Not much.

So I pushed the door, slowly, carefully, so it didn't creak.

The door squeals!

Who the fuck is this? I got a gun!

The voice comes from the other bedroom. I'm standing in the living room. It's looking tidy with two suitcases neatly arranged near the sofa. This isn't a burglary.

Who the fuck are you? I scream at the bedroom door at the top of my lungs, trying to sound scary. What are you doing in my apartment??

Cursing in English doesn't come naturally to me. I don't speak enough to practice. I can tell my French accent makes me sound too effeminate to scare anyone.

A little skinny darkskin dude with big eyes and broad shoulders comes out of the guest room in a tight T-shirt and baggy pants.

Who the fuck are you?

He mimes my voice and accent and smiles.

The tension in the room drops, but I'm still on my guard.

You're a nigga? A French nigga? Ain't that some shit. I wasn't expecting that. Hi, I'm Miles.

He sticks out his right hand for me to shake.

I'm looking at this little dude with his little hand, and I'm trying to calm down. To stop shaking with fear and adrenaline. It's my roommate.

Miles Davis, right? I'm Gilbert Chevalier.

Nice to meet you, man. You can stop shaking now, nigga. Damn. The school didn't tell you I was coming?

You were supposed to be here months ago.

Yes, but I was on tour in Europe. Shit was beautiful, man. Juilliard understood. I'm here now. Gotta get this degree to make my pops happy. Is everyone at Columbia as square as you? Where you from, anyway?

Haiti, I say, with pride, finally shaking his hand.

Haiti? *Pas mal, pas mal.*

Tu parles français?

I never meet Americans who speak French! This Miles Davis was sloppy with closing doors, but he was turning out all right.

No, nigga, I don't speak French. I'm from St. Louis. But I love Paris. I've been there a few times and played the best shows. Picked up a few lines. Not too much, just enough to pick up French women.

Mon dieu, I thought, shaking my head in disbelief.

Suddenly, someone was pounding on our apartment door. Miles jumped up into boxing stance. I was like, what now?

Miles! A woman screamed.

A strong woman. That door might not survive another blow.

I know you're in there. I followed your ass from Smalls'. Miles! Open up!

Oh shit! Miles said. That's Veronica. I been hiding from that bitch all week.

Miles sprinted to his room. Don't tell her I'm here!

More pounding on the door. Miles!

How did I go from church service to the circus of Miles Davis? I opened the door.

She was magnificent. Tall, sooooo tall, taller than me! and skinny, all legs and breasts and a sophisticated and hip New York sister's hair style. Okay, Miles. Salute. You have good taste in women.

Can I help you?

You're not Miles.

Non. Je m'appelle Gilbert. You?

Oh, tu parles français?

Ouais, suis d'Haïti. Toi?

Côte d'Ivoire.

Super. Parlez français me manquais. Tu habites ici?

I had nothing more clever to say. I'd been loyal to Aurélie for many months now, and my flirt game had faded.

She wasn't trying to flirt.

Il n'est pas la, I said, sincerely.

She believed me.

Do you know when he's coming home? she said, switching to English to conjure some toughness, but it was a heartbroken woman's voice talking. No matter the language, the frustration of thwarted love is universally awful. I glimpse the little girl she must have been not too long ago in Africa, which I imagine looks and feels a lot like Haiti but on a much grander scale. Verdant, lively, muddy, sexy, severe, depending on how close you live to the deserts or not. Haiti has no deserts and probably too many waterfalls for its own good. Yet I resisted shooting my shot.

Tell you the truth, I don't know when Miles will be home again. You know Miles. He could be gigging in Montreal or Vienna right now and not tell anyone. He's an unreliable little bastard.

She almost smiled. She sized me up, probably wondering how much more or less reliable I was than Miles.

Veronique, she said. My name is Veronique. But everyone calls me Vero. You can find me dancing on Broadway.

With that, she turned and headed toward the stairs. There was a swagger to her perfectly formed ass and long, bowed legs when she walked away that I took as I sign that she knew I was checking her out. She was indeed as fine from the back as she was from the front. I shook my head and smiled and closed the door. Women, man, *incroyable mais vrai, toujours.*

Unreliable, huh, nigga?

Miles was standing in front of his room dressed in a sharp navy suit and brandishing his trumpet like a spear.

Grab your coat and let's go. I'll show you what I'm reliable for.

Outside, the New York City early winter night was cold and blustery. Gusts of wind attacked us like hoodlums, slashed my face and neck and exposed my inability to deal with the cold like ninjas slicing through a kimono. I couldn't close my coat tightly enough. *Mon dieu.* Now I remembered why I avoided going out at night most of the time. During New York winters, gusts of wind and chill assaulted you on every street corner. I'd prefer to be mugged by good old-fashioned hoodlums. But Miles was solar. He greeted everyone with a hardy smile like they were old friends. Old folks, young folks, maitre d's and swank folks in mink coats, drug dealers and shop owners, even cops. I struggled to keep up with his little legs. He was my age and had been in the city only a little bit longer, but that shiny trumpet of his had given him some fame. It had opened the city up to him to a staggering degree. In the streets, he often had his arms open and mouth open to drink in his good fortune. He embraced his fame with open arms. And people, the world, embraced him in return. When he bent down to embrace a junkie shaking in a doorway and chat with him, I thought it odd. When the junkie got up and dusted off the giant case he was using as a pillow to join us, I was even more surprised.

Gilbert Chevalier, meet my man John Coltrane. John's the greatest saxophonist in the world, no disrespect to Bird. John doesn't know it yet. But Bird knows it. We're going to make the best jazz music the world has and will ever hear.

We walked into Minton's Playhouse, the jazz club. It was hot and musky, crowded, rowdy, and reeking of sex. The boys' coats were taken from them as they walked to the stage. Dizzy and his band cleared the way. I didn't know Miles could be that quiet for that long. I took a seat in a booth. Everyone around me lit up cigarettes as if on cue. The band unsheathed their instruments. The pianist cracked his fingers and sat like a king on a throne. Miles's trumpet took on a glow that could only be described as saintly. When he finished his sly opening verse and ceded to Coltrane, Trane's solo swung so gently, so confidently, so purely, it sounded like he was channeling the best dream of all time. I'd heard drum solos in Haiti that sounded good, but this night, a cat named Max Roach was drumming well enough to raise the dead. He was steady, strong, and clever, signaling black power, somehow, and suggesting that the black dirt in our black hands, and the black muscles that beat back so much bad faith and bad luck, held powers unforeseen. The world was ours, if you just listened to the next solo by the scintillating young black men on this stage. They were instruments, living, breathing, heaven-sent instruments meant to suffer but smile through it all, for we held invisible blessings in our melanin.

Dear Aurélie,

I discovered the most incredible music recently. Miles Davis, my roommate, and his quintet are amazing! To hear John Coltrane play that saxophone on a dark and chilly night in Harlem was to hear something akin to the notes God listens to when He's sitting with his angels, enjoying a good drink and marveling at humanity's occasional successes at not fucking things up too much. To listen to Coltrane play on a tune called "All Blues" is to appreciate that my blues for you, the unavailable love of my life, for Elizabeth, my unloved wife, Jackie and my family, okay maybe not the family, but Haiti and our compatriots, and all the other blues in the world, were temporary, ephemeral, for love was everywhere and solid and certain. We know it. We knew it. We just pay too much attention to the pain from missing things. Both Miles and John are masters of a sleight of hand. Their first notes may sound sweet, seem to promise romance, but urgency is often their main message, Miles with his reedy confidence and John with his loop de loops and insistent hilarity. These are angry young black men, true, but these guys are above all also passionate, quite heavily emotional men. They dare to blanket audiences with their big hearts and seemingly bottomless ability to please us and fuck with us, and cry with us and cry for us, just so, just enough, to make us believe they love us.

I know I wasn't the type to gush about music like this before. But watching these brilliant musicians shine as individuals and also as a band is blowing my mind every night. I suppose they're reconnecting me to the things I loved about playing football on a team. A group of individuals with unique talents and voices coming together to pursue a common goal: scoring goals and not giving up goals.

I miss the game, Aurélie. But I'm staying focused on my mission here. Becoming a diligent accountant and technocrat. Sounds like eating sand, don't it? But that's okay. Miles and his band and the other jazz musicians and artists I'm discovering around town are exciting. My turn to share my talents with the world will come, won't it? I hope so. Meantime, these artists got me dreaming!

Dreams are good things, chérie. Real good things.

What are you dreaming about these days?

Your dreamboat,
Gil

Dear Aurélie,

Remember Veronique, that sad ex-girlfriend of Miles's I told you about? I wished Vero was there with us some of those nights at Harlem nightspots, when Miles and his quintet buried us in their loving blues. Maybe their musical blues would soothe her blues, like they were soothing mine. Then again, she probably had too many of those nights listening to the Miles Davis quintet display enough soul power to enthrall the entire planet. Loving geniuses like these leads to heartbreak, yours and theirs! Ours? I was one of them once, when I played foot. When I looked around the enthralled, infatuated crowds around the halls where jazz was played, I saw a thousand Veroniques, like when I played football in a packed stadium in downtown Port-au-Prince. Then again, I saw poor Vero's mistake too. Women and men who loved these musicians' limitless ability to share their loves, voices, and passions, a love filled with confident wit, they mistook the songs and the notes as being played and sung uniquely for them. Jazz is so intense, seemingly ripped from musicians' ribs. I can't blame its lovers for feeling loved. Something about watching a man or woman spill her spleen on a stage makes you feel intimately connected to them. You feel cradled by their seemingly bottomless big hearts, but it is art, not their actual hearts! I felt like screaming that to the fans falling over themselves in these nightclubs. Lena Horne, Billie Holiday, they had that effect on men and women too. Violently seductive blues. Their searing vulnerability, their knowing smiles, these musicians seemed ultra-human. But their lovers soon discovered these musicians were human, barely adult; junkies, gamblers, and oversharers. They were children with adult physiques, born to play music like inventive children for a living, but players are jesters too, aren't they? Aren't we?

Love us at your own peril. Look at me, blurring my athletic frustrations with these artists in bloom. Their limitations reminded me of the man I was when I played. Their fickle, fragile mood, easily swayed by the last flattery, the first unsolicited hug, it clashed with the boundlessness of their art and the finite duration of their primes as stars. Pity to those who mistake one for the other. Genius in one thing doesn't always translate to genius humanity. Football players can tell you that, right? Aurélie. Because we participate in so many hard-fought matches that finish with no goals. A draw. A hard-won tie. An oxymoron, but quite akin to life itself. A piece of art's mere existence in itself lights up a scoreboard. Every book is a miracle of a few hundred pages. But football is life. Some days you don't score despite trying your manic best, and that's okay. Actually, it's not okay. You feel awful after those games—and their collection of what-if scenarios—for days afterward till the next game.

How can you perform so well after spending a day sleeping in the streets high on heroin? I asked Coltrane late one night. It was the next morning. We were feasting over breakfast at

Tom's Diner on the Upper West Side. The cold outside felt like the air was shooting daggers through our bodies. I don't think I can survive many of these New York City winters. My ankles felt brittle from the winds cutting through my socks. The cold slapped my wrists, and now they felt like a saw had gone through them to try to cut off my hands. I needed better gloves.

John shrugged.

I don't know.

Miles smiled to himself.

Do you know why, Miles?

I do. But so what?

Funny guy, right?

I hope you're well, Aurélie.

Je t'embrasse fort.

Yours,
Gilbert

PART II

GLORIOSO, MINEIRÃO

We have a tendency to forget, but we are eternal children when we play football.

—KYLIAN MBAPPÉ, FRENCH FOOTBALL STAR

9

JOGO BONITO IN CENTRAL PARK

I was on a date that wasn't a date in Central Park late that winter when my first true love came roaring back into my life. My date was sweet, steady, charming, her eyes sparkled, even in repose. A senior, but so peripatetic, she seemed younger than me sometimes, everything seemed together yet also volatile with her, success seemingly preordained, from perfect grades, internships, to graduate school, yet she was overflowing with dreams and ambitions and restlessness. Whatever her parents wanted for her, I didn't know, she didn't want to talk about them much. She was free of the expectations of anyone other than herself, and her standards were high. *Impressionante!* I thought. *Elle était exigeante avec elle même d'une manière presque violente. C'était beau. Elle était belle, bien sûr. Trop belle pour moi de ne pas avoir des fantasies de nous ensemble. Mais elle s'en foutait de sa beauté. Et la mienne aussi? Je ne savais pas.* Her name was Francoise, and she was spectacularly black, pearl-like, her skin was the smoothest I'd ever seen in my life. I wanted to sleep with her just to see if she woke up as flawlessly. Her name was French, but she was from Chicago. And she was heading to Togo for the summer, part family reasons, part volunteering as a medical assistant in hospitals. She desperately wanted to become one of the rare black women to graduate from Harvard Medical School.

Going to Africa is key to making my application stand out, she said. Africa can be overwhelming and dangerous, but it will be fun, she added in her singsong voice, almost convincing me that a summer in an African rainforest filled with mosquitos and warring Christians, Muslims, and former colonial masters could be fun, as if African spiders and snakes and parrots are as fun as the coconut trees and stray dogs that were waiting for me in the Caribbean. My incentive, she proposed, was the fact that those bright brown eyes of hers didn't light up for every man, and those eyes could become softer toward me in ways that were marvelous and deep.

But I never got the nerve to ask her about that, and why we hung out so much, but during those hot winter nights of jazz in Harlem, Francoise barely glanced at another man when she was with me, not Miles when he tried to seduce her with his penetrating coal-black stare, and not even beautifully tragic Coltrane, even after the show that one night when Coltrane and his sax gave the world a glimpse of heaven *en vivo*, with a solo that was putrid and sacred and hair-raising and oh so amazing. That night, Coltrane raised the roof at Smalls' Paradise, thrilling madly a crowd of connoisseurs, dealers, pimps, the mayor, a senator, a congressman, and tycoons, so many tycoons. I learned to recognize them. New York City tycoons in 1950 were different from Haitian tycoons, not because they wore monocles and top hats or anything like that, though some of them still did, but because their ladies wore mink coats all the time, giving the impression they wore nothing else underneath, even though the club was hot as fuck. The rich man's wife kept her mink coat, the only things she seemed to wear beyond that were pearl necklaces and high heels. The black women in the clubs didn't wear minks, yet many of them were tycoons' girlfriends, even the smart ones, even Francoise, which was disappointing, but such was the fauna and flora of Manhattan, the tycoons sported blondes in minks as arm candy and also as a form of promise to their mistresses, both current and future, that they could have mink coats too someday, if they played their cards right and let them have their way with them during lunchtimes or when the missus left town with the kids to visit her parents, the young black women giggled at the idea when a tycoon gave them a wink as he raised a glass of champagne with his crew, but the experienced sisters were contemptuous, Gil could feel their spines harden and their eyes frost up during those toasts. They knew the deception inside the smile of the rich man, they stared daggers at the motherfuckers, not cold enough to kill them, but maybe, hopefully, induce a heart attack, so their flunkies could cry for a nurse to help, and the sisters, many of whom were indeed nurses, would sneer and leave the club by walking over the writhing body of this or that stricken former lover forever.

Just then a theatrical drumroll summoned our collective attentions. Its boom shook our tables and asses. The song was a sneak peak of John Coltrane's album in progress, *A Love Supreme.* "Pursuance" was the title, John had told me. The song was an alarm call, he said. I know you getting into the God thing, Gil. Going to church and all that. That's pretty cool. But you too cool about it. God gotta be chased, my nigga. Pursued!

After Elvin Jones kicked off "Pursuance" with his drum

solo, Coltrane let McCoy Tyner get loose. No one let McCoy solo much, but he needed this solo badly, he was in bad shape, not from heroin or booze or gambling, he was suffering a worse fate than that. His lady, Dara Scorpio, a brainy beauty freshly arrived from Atlanta, had left him for a tycoon.

I want to see what being with a reliable man feels like, she told him on her way out the door, and the greatest pianist and tempo keeper in the jazz world fell apart, his heart reduced to scattered keys in a dumpster.

But I'm Mr. Reliable, McCoy pleaded. Everyone calls me that.

Not on rent day, nigga, Dara shot back.

Funny as that line was, I felt unlucky to witness that scene, during a random visit at McCoy's place. After Dara slammed the door in the face of his begging, McCoy looked at me with bleeding eyes and said, Can you believe that shit??? I loved that bitch! I loved her to death, man.

And then he asked me to lend him some bread to pay the rent. I did. Yeah, I did. I had learned that when you're friends with musicians, writers, and actors, occasionally lending them bread for their rent is an occupational hazard.

That night, McCoy played with elegant fury on "Pursuance." When Coltrane's solo came, he brought a form of rage to the prayerful song, an angry faith, ten minutes of wild incantation, he sounded like the wailing that must have taken place in heaven when Jesus expired on the cross. Abruptly, Coltrane interrupted his *cri de coeur* to plunge the crowd into melancholia, his vulnerability triggering ours to shiver. He seemed to reveal the hushed mood that greeted Jesus after he died and reminded the crowd how far and feeble we were compared with Him, and that the holy place was out of our reach, no matter the charms of power, fame, mink coats, wealth, and sexy smiles. In that tender moment, as Coltrane played solemn note after solemn note, the crowded room in Smalls' Paradise got woozy like a boxer hammered by haymakers. We needed smelling salts, or relief, like we sensed the coming joy in the world in the return of Jesus, if we submitted to Him and Trane's quiet tenor saxophone prayer. Coltrane was using his industrial-strength lungs and love of God to tell us, no, make us, feel, He hath risen, God was among us, God was us. God *could* be us if we felt what Trane was feeling in his soul. I looked around and saw a sea of mouths agape, cigarettes unlit and dangling on lips, or burning to a stub, drinks unserved, and undrunk. God was in the building, and Coltrane's sweeping, sweet playing was a gentle call to alert, making devils uncomfortable. Heathens were momentarily paralyzed. The faithful were in awe. Atheists lost their hard-ons. I wanted to dance. Francoise told me not to touch her by leaning away. The song had annoyed her. She didn't like Coltrane much. Too relentless, she said. It can't be music in conversation with God and heaven if it suffocates me, she added. *Trop débordant de passion*, she said, smiling, as if accusing me of something. She was hanging out with me to improve her French before going to Africa, full stop, nothing more, I now had to concede, not because she considered me particularly unattractive or square, but because I didn't pass an unspoken audition, hell, I wasn't invited to audition for the role of her leading man. We would never French kiss, I accepted, which was a shame since that's the most important way to speak French. But that's all right. I couldn't explain why, but the more I hung out in sexy jazz clubs, listening to Miles's coolly romantic songs and Coltrane's melodramatic prayers, the less horny I got, I grew melancholic, which led me to think about Haiti, and Aurélie, and my family, my unpredictable and loving family, the talismanic powers of money and power, represented by white people, all was well in my life until white people showed up, but it's not like white people were ever truly not in our lives. In New York City, their authority *et main mise* was unavoidable. In Port-au-Prince, they were everywhere too. But Port-au-Prince seemed very far away during those sweaty, thrilling nights of vagabondage in Harlem.

Faces are becoming hard to remember, I wrote to Aurélie that night.

I conjure them, and they evaporate. My memories are being consumed by the vivid jazz tunes, maybe the version of myself I saw in the eyes of people back home is becoming harder for me to remember. I feel so free in New York City. Wandering in and out of people's lives, discovering and loving jazz. The music is becoming a real obsession. Meeting new people all the time, not stressing the meaning of these relationships. I feel so free from the rigid social codes of Haiti. New York City is as class-conscious as Haiti, don't get me wrong. The thing is, here I don't care about class and social climbing. I'm just passing through for a few years before returning home to you, Aurélie.

I do feel like I am changing. I have to be honest. This city, the music, the high color of the folks. They are changing me slowly into someone new, someone who is an amalgamation of things, cultures, voices. Columbia, Harlem, Miles. The jazz. The grandiosity of everything and everyone, no matter their standing in life. To be honest, the old Gilbert is fading. Disappearing. Fast.

Gil remembers how he felt after writing that letter to Aurélie. It was the first time he kinda lied to her. What he didn't say is he used to pray for Aurélie to stay loyal to him, ridiculous as that sounds since he was married to another woman and living in a different country, but he was starting to wonder if it was fair to ask her or anyone who knew him back in Haiti to hold on to him. Who would she be staying loyal to? She could be faithful, he thought, but to what? And for what? Gil was the weak one of the two of them, a citizen of multiple cultures being formatted by the many subcultures of America. When Gil was home alone and still melancholic and horny, his frustrations led him to blame his beloved for his wandering id. In those moments, he knew he was changing but he also realized Aurélie could be changing too, not only because of his physical distance, but because she was equally young, beautiful, and brave. Yet he clung to her. They had an understanding. They had a passion. They had one amazing night (and morning). They were Haitians in love, a people bedeviled perpetually by a maelstrom of melodramatic politics, pride, and precarity; when Haitians loved, they loved completely and irrationally, love for them was not just a feeling, it was not for the weak of heart, it was the last armor before death. Life at its strongest. It was the bomb of all bombs, unjust, mad, all-encompassing. His *coup de foudre* for Aurélie was inappropriate. It was fun. It was theirs, solid as a diamond. Or a mirage. He was too young to know the difference. No alternative to this passion yet existed.

Except for the day football reentered my life, he recalled. That day in Central Park, during a walk with Francoise on a not yet chilly fall afternoon, a football came roaring out of nowhere and smacked me in the face. The ball struck me so hard and squarely that I was thrown feetfirst in the air until my body lifted and became parallel to the ground before falling with a splat. Flat on my back. Instead of getting upset, I looked at the ball lovingly and laughed.

I missed you too, baby.

Another day I would have wondered why Francoise didn't bend down and ask if I was okay. Didn't she care about me? Amazed at how little she cared. But the taste of the leather ball surrounded by grass was delicious, the most addictive flavor of the favorite meal of my childhood. Football! I was triggered. My feet and instincts for football were reactivated.

Hey, man, I'm sorry.

The player with the errant foot stood over me, a large shadow framed by the bright late afternoon sun. As he apologized, a dozen other players joined him, surrounding me. I was lying on the ground with a goofy grin on my face. I did feel a little woozy from the surprise blow of the football, which might have explained the concerned looks on their faces. Maybe I looked concussed too. The players were Latinos and Europeans and Africans, swarthy and barely washed. Immigrants! My people. I was so busy making friends with Americans and becoming American, I had neglected my tribe, the people who glanced away at church on Sundays, but showed up every Sunday, people who barely spoke English and when they did, they spoke English with foreign accents. Delighted to live in New York City by day, but at night they suffocated with loneliness and exhaustion from the work it takes to earn American dollars and community. These men and boys and their worried companions apologized to me in a chorus of accents, some I knew well, the burr of German, the high pitches of French, the softness of Spanish, the mushiness of Portuguese. The nervousness of Swahili. These accents had become familiar to me over the months in Harlem. There was fear in some of their faces too, for that, also, was a standard feature of every new immigrant interaction with people they believed to be locals. Please don't call the police on me for my mistake, they said without saying, Please don't make a fuss. And definitely please don't retaliate and try to hurt me. For all they knew I was black American, and eruptions of random violence are essential to the myth of black Americans, as it is with most Americans, they are impulsive gangsters to most foreigners, even when they aren't, but colonialism and American history being inflected with genocidal tendencies as it was, the savagery of black Americans, especially in New York City, was a popular and persistent idea, for it covered up or justified the rampant violence of the police and other authorities, therefore, like all smart black men since the dawn of this bullshit, I knew how to disarm the tension. I smiled.

You need one more player? I said.

The players were visibly relieved by my accented English. I was one of them!

Si, they said.

Oui.

Ja!

Tak!

Sim!

Asante.

Give me a hand then.

Vamos!

I left my books and coat and woman and romantic worries behind in the crimson-orange Manhattan twilight and never looked back. Football was my jazz. It was showtime. I ran to the pitch, on the Sheep Meadow, a large flat swath of Central Park grass, with my new friends, with the lightness of boyhood, and soon we became more than friends, we became teammates. All I could think of was the ball and my teammates' feet and their timing and speed and skills with and without the ball, gauging, always assessing, moving, becoming available, feeling the defenses defending, protecting my space, creating new spaces, opportunities, communicating that feeling, constantly communicating with our bodies and hands, sometimes eyes, rarely words, words are for novices, but the good ones catch up quick, first we were a dozen boys and men, running in sync like a herd of gazelles, a ballet of defenders and attackers and midfielders, bracketed by goalkeepers, chasing the other team when they had the ball in one direction, and, after a turnover, running hard in the other direction, sometimes I felt like I ran all the way down to Wall Street chasing that damn ball, other times, while leaping as high as I could to try to get my head on a cross, my afro probably looked like it sat atop the missile my body had become, grazing the moon. In a few weeks our five-a-side games morphed into proper eleven-a-sides in front of thirsty crowds at the Polo Grounds in upper Manhattan.

After one of those matches, when our team, the Brookhattans—yes, the name is terrible, what the hell is a Brookhattan?—won a victory against the supposedly formidable New York Mets, where I scored a couple of goals so easily I felt fresh enough to play another ninety-minute match, my football bestie, José, signaled I had a visitor. She was waiting down the corridor.

She was sultry, but stolid. She was reading me, no, no, she had read me already. Jesus, another scarily intelligent beautiful woman. My friends met the easiest, simplest women routinely. Not me. Because of Elizabeth and Aurélie and my mother, I'd come to equate intelligence in a beautiful woman with an ability to love me and let me go too easily. Way too easily.

Bonjour, I said.

Pleased to meet you, Mr. Chevalier, she said. I'm Léa Killdare.

Up close she was skinny and a tad too pale. Yet prettier and smarter than I thought, with the easy authority of the wealthy.

Good game, she added.

Oh, she liked football? Her stock started going up in my eyes. She was not wearing a mink coat, but I could tell she had an old man. I didn't know what the play was here. Football groupies in New York City were normally immigrants too, wives and girlfriends and relatives of former players, or newly arrived friends of wives and girlfriends and relatives of players. Curious college students didn't stick around after games. And Léa seemed American. Americans, I don't know about them. I had no problem with them, don't get me wrong, but I'd gotten used to the pleasures of hanging out with fellow outsiders, and a certain *méfiance* of locals seeped into me. When you're a relatively charming immigrant, locals can quickly bring you deep into their intimacy and abruptly discard you too, seemingly on a whim. You were there, but you weren't really there. Then you were made to feel no longer wanted. Or needed. They were done with you. Their curiosity satiated. Your person was a discarded husk. I had been spared this embarrassment so far, but those wounds were common chatter among my teammates and their families after a few drinks. I feared my turn was Léa. Immigrants needed each other's sympathy and favors too much to be too fickle in our relationships. Among immigrants I felt valued, necessary. It was a nice, new feeling. In Haiti, I was valued too, but mostly for my family name, without doing much of anything else to earn my place in the society. Without earning a role on the island. In the scrum of New York City's community of first-generation, not-quite-minted Americans, being a reliable friend, a teammate on the field and in life, was golden. With Americans and America itself, it takes a while to get your footing, to become certain of where you stand and why they like you, if they like you at all, and if they do, how long their interests in your charming accent and culture will last.

My father wants to meet you, Léa said.

Her friendliness had been replaced by a serious tone. She looked like a minx, but she had gravity. Didn't see that coming.

What a shame, I said. This was only a business visit.

No, Mr. Chevalier, it's much, much bigger than that.

That evening in Manhattan, Léa Killdare and her father surprised me with an offer I would not refuse. They invited me to join the U.S. men's soccer team preparing to play the World Cup tournament in Brazil. A footballer's dream. I'm not American, but I'll suit up for them to play in a World Cup in a heartbeat! To play against the best players in the world under the most intense lights will be exciting. Haiti doesn't have a team, but I'll rep us wherever I go.

10

ONE–NIL

Back home in Haiti, one of the two most important women in Gil's life made a life-changing discovery.

I'm pregnant?

Scheisse.

Elizabeth Chevalier sat in disbelief in the doctor's office, staring deep into Dr. Smith's eyes, hoping to see a glint of a joke in their hazel gleam.

No, it's not a joke, he said. Congrats to you and your husband. Your first baby is on its way.

In a daze, Elizabeth walked out of the doctor's office in the glittering morning sun toward the midday traffic of Grand Rue. Located off Grand Rue, near Librairie Auguste, Dr. Smith's clinic was discreet. He had an anglophone name. As a result, his medical practice wasn't popular with the Chevaliers and their friends in the Haitian elite. Her new bestie, Coco, helped her find him. She needed discretion. She wasn't sure she wanted to keep the baby.

How can you be so sure you're pregnant? Coco said. The morning sickness could be a flu. He's been gone for so long.

I just know, Coco. Something about the way he filled me up the first time.

Really?

I swear, his semen flooded through my entire body. I was afraid it would pour out of my eyes!

You're funny, Elizabeth.

For a German. You can say it.

Girl, you stopped being German when you climbed up that mango tree that time and brought down a mango you ate barefoot sitting in the grass.

It's true, Elizabeth has been transitioning from haughty young German to laid-back Caribbean woman more easily than she expected. How does a white woman blend into the blackest and proudest nation on earth? She eats mangos barefoot, of course, literally and metaphorically. She was sporty and cocky and refined when she wanted to be, like typical Haitian women, but she also let her hair down and listened, *listened*, in sisterhood. Ever ambitious, she already wanted to transition from white girl to black woman, a bridge way too far, but she was who she was and doing the impossible should be easy too, she assumed. She couldn't understand why she couldn't become a black woman, but she couldn't, even the white people who *were* born in Haiti to generations of whites couldn't become black, they were called *blanc pays*, native, cool, but still very white, suspect, so Elizabeth, who was not native and also from a country so uncool that it once fancied itself the whitest of all time, had no chance, but she wasn't one to accept barriers, whether in languages, dances, academics, music, sports, anything, so the mystery of the divide between her and a force that seemed to generate fervor akin to the divine among the men and women, boys and girls, around her had to be understood, had to be mastered and brought to submission. If I'm as smart as I'm supposed to be, I'm going to overcome this challenge too, she told herself. Once in a while she'd be honest with herself and also wonder, what did it mean to be a black woman anyway? What did they have that she didn't have? Could it really be as simple as their darker skin pigmentation, spongy hair, and history of ably nurturing the builders of Western civilization?

Of course it was.

But people like Elizabeth had trouble accepting the obvious. Fortunately, she was also smart enough to be unafraid to ask stupid questions. How do I become accepted as Haitian, Coco? How do I become Haitian?

Tu ne peux pas, Elizabeth.

Humor me, Coco.

The view of the ocean from Coco's house in Fontamara was dreamy, a shimmering blue-green, the white sand of the beach framed the waters like hands cupping an offering to the gods, and the way the water stretched far into the ocean and disappeared suggested the ocean was a pipeline, which gave Haiti the feeling of an island apart from the world, yet also a source of life for the world, known and unknown, an alternative universe in itself, till Coco brought Elizabeth back to reality.

Well, you have a few things going for you to become Haitian. For one, you married a Haitian man, never an easy move.

Elizabeth's right hand stroked her pregnant belly, the memory of how she probably got pregnant slowly making her sweat.

You're about to have a Haitian baby that you'll raise by yourself, like many Haitian women have done since the dawn of time since slavers had the charming policy of often separating fathers from their children and women. On top of that, you live in loud and messy Port-au-Prince.

I'm looking good, according to your checklist.

Not really.

What?

You have to have money problems.

Oh.

You have to dream big to be Haitian. Chronically. For example, you have to have dreams of escaping Haiti, which you either sabotage continually, or you just never find the means to execute. Is that your case?

Merde.

Last but not least, you have to live and love like each day and love is your last.

Why?

That's how we do here. Think about it. For two hundred years, our men had to live with the fear that the slavemaster would separate him, or worse, from the love of his life as soon as he got wind of their love. The legacy of that horror seems to be that when we get a whiff of love around the country, we become irrationally inseparable. Obsessed. Which is maddening. Definitely not healthy for everyone, not even Haitians.

I could work with that!

You think you can. But you won't really know until a Haitian man falls in love with you. No offense.

None taken.

He will seek to own your heart and devour your body with his attention and appetite for lust and passion, and when you believe you've given him all the love and passion and time and compassion you have to give, and you're exhausted and strained from his constant attention and demands, he will double down. He will ask you for more love. The hole in his soul is bigger than you thought. He needs more love and passion and compassion from you to fill it than you have. Soon you will find more of you wasn't enough either. You'll try harder. You'll find depths of love you didn't know you had to keep it going.

Wow! That sounds heavy.

You people are crazy, Elizabeth wanted to say. But she had been hanging out with Haitians long enough by this point to know that the two words, *you people*, coming out of her pert pink lips would banish her to the land of *mépris* for a while, an unpleasant and ever-ready penalty box for white people who got too comfortable around black folk. Besides, little did Coco know, Elizabeth had already met a lovely Haitian gentleman caller.

At the party after her wedding. Late in the night, or early in the morning, she had crawled down from the ceiling where she had been dancing with so many boys and girls for so long for so much fun and so much sweat that she needed a break. The air on the balcony of the mansion overlooking the stars gathered over Port-au-Prince was fresh and clean. The stars seemed to sparkle just for her, the beautiful bride whose husband had disappeared. The stars uplifted her. A sensation she never experienced staring at the sky from the balcony of her family's mansion in Munich. It rained or snowed too much at night in Germany for stargazing. And it was cold. It didn't take Elizabeth Chevalier, née Schattenham, long to go from homesick Nazi teen to wannabe Caribbean woman with a taste for the luxuries of Haitian life. Teenagers can do that. Germany was for her parents, she was starting to think. She could reinvent herself in Haiti in ways they couldn't imagine.

They were already in bed, the losers. These Haitians really know how to party. They know how to live. They are so hot, and she is so thirsty.

You could use a drink, a man with a gravelly, courtly voice said behind her.

He was small, very black, and handsome despite the owlish glasses that reminded her of her family's accountant. He handed her a glittering glass of champagne and didn't bother trying to smile. She could see clearly the salacious interest in his eyes and the restrained glee in his voice. It was transparent despite his scholarly mien and dark-rum voice. His lust was naked and vivid in a more intriguing way than the smiling and groping young men she had been dancing with after walking down the aisle with Gilbert and losing him to his buddies and the music of Jazz des Jeunes.

Thank you . . .

Doctor. Doctor Duvalier. You can call me François. I also dabble in politics. I accompanied the president here tonight.

Oh la, la, nice to meet you, François.

Hearing her say his first name seemed to tickle him. Not many people get that privilege, she could tell. The doctor liked being called doctor very much.

What kind of doctor are you?

Come to my cabinet at Hotel Karibe on Monday, lunchtime, and I'll show you.

Why not tomorrow, Herr Doctor?

No, François said firmly. You're going to need all of tomorrow to recover from today's festivities. You're going to need all your energy for your visits with me.

Elizabeth grew aroused by this disquietingly bold old man. She was almost annoyed she couldn't leave with him on the spot to learn what sexual delights he had in mind for her in his cabinet in a hotel. She changed the subject.

I didn't know we had any doctors on the guest list. Then again, I don't know anyone here other than the family.

That must feel odd to not know anyone at your own wedding party.

Elizabeth relished the question. No one had much sympathy for her since she arrived in Haiti, not even her own family. Everyone just ordered her around, sending her to and fro, smiling at her like she was an idiot. Her gilded standing and all the fawning didn't leave room for her to share her shock, awe, and anxieties with anyone.

At the Karibe Hotel, that Monday, two days later, in a large room with the shades drawn, the sex with Dr. Duvalier blew her mind. Elizabeth found herself making love with a man who was not her new husband in a way she had never experienced at all. François Duvalier tied her wrists with black ropes to the bedposts and then stretched her legs and spread them wide open and then he tied her ankles to the bed with black ropes. They didn't talk much. He was a careful, attentive man, and he took great pleasure and care in the minutiae of gagging and binding her to a bed before making love to her. He didn't blindfold her, though. He seemed to want her to see what he was doing to her, how he moved carefully to bind her, and how he smelled her and her excitement, how much he savored the act of dominating her. She needed to feel possessed by someone who actually cared about her, and there was a tenderness here too. He clearly had a very specific method for sharing affection that made her feel like she was his. He smiled so broadly with joy when he penetrated her, his toothiness was endearing, and his cry and moans thrilled her to orgasm. She never knew she could experience such intense pleasures from doing nothing. She was helpful in her helplessness. For the busybody that she was, visiting her good doctor in his dark hotel room would be the highlight of her week for many years. Oddly, his domination soothed her, and, unknown to her, his appetite for the submission of others would spread wildly across the entire nation.

11

CIRANDAR

The world went green when the plane entered Brazilian airspace. I had never seen such vast expanses of green before: green trees, plains, jungles, and plants; neither had my Mexican, European, and American country-boy teammates. Every shade of emerald possible, shades of green that seemed unreal, and shades of green that were impossibly beautiful, shades of abundant verdancy that the perpetual golden sunshine of Brazil struck just right from sunrise to sunset to keep us giddy, awestruck, and feeling perpetually on the verge of finding treasures and sensual pleasures. Everything and everyone seemed improbably attractive, framed as they were by so many reflections of gold and green, nature overpowering concrete, creating a rich, sacred mood, making us feel like Adam in Eden, Eve was bound to materialize, of course she would, many Eves, simple, barely dressed, yet striking women of all ages appeared, as if on cue, as if fallen from trees, or risen from the earth, the gentle, ripe soil we were walking on, which is more ground than asphalt, these Eves seemed ready to assuage our confusion and delight our curiosity. Ethereal yet solid. These women and girls were no mirages. And they held no apples in their hands. Before we could begin to engage their smiles, this forest of a nation had to be tamed by our overwhelmed senses. So many types of green! Green-green. Poised green, dark green, happy green, pretty green, mountain green, for there were mountains, oh, there were mountains, they surrounded us for as far as the eyes could see after we walked out of the airport. The mountains were heavy and hulking, but lush, bountiful, and pregnant with life.

Big life. Brazil is one of the largest and most populated countries in the world, I could feel life teeming around us. The geography books at Low Library told me a lot about Brazil as I prepared for this trip, but the books couldn't come close to helping me grasp the sense of grandeur and immensity of the country after the bus ride from the airport brought us to the middle of the central plaza, the Circuito Cultural Praça da Liberdade, for the first time. The state in Brazil we found ourselves in was called Minas Gerais. The words meant General Mines in Portuguese, said Ron Banks, our host. A mysterious Jamaican who made a fortune in the mines, he owned the Kingston, the grand hotel we would be staying in while competing in the first round of the football World Cup, the first such tournament since the Second World War ended. Minas is filled with mines producing all manner of commodities and precious metals for the world, he said. I hope you find its history of resourcefulness inspiring.

The organizers and the press in New York City and Washington told us the tournament was a big deal. They also told us the United States of America was expected to be the worst team in the tournament. We got in only because the war destroyed most of Europe and many good European sides couldn't afford to field teams, or field enough healthy male bodies to lace up boots to play, and since the war left the U.S. nakedly the most powerful and wealthy country in the world, it was welcome in the small selective club of football-playing nations. America became that rich, uncouth friend you had to invite out because he was exceedingly grateful to be among the cool and often eager to pick up the tab. The world let it fund the United Nations, the North Atlantic Treaty Organization, and the football World Cup, among other bulwarks for peace in a world hungover from terrible wars, plural, for the Second World War was not a sequel of the First World War. That war began in 1914 and technically ended in 1918, but intellectually raged on through the 1920s and '30s till it climaxed with gas chambers, Pearl Harbor, and nuclear fucking bomb explosions that could have ignited the atmosphere and destroyed the entire planet. Nuclear bombs could have destroyed the world. The nuclear bombs could have destroyed the world. Those damn nuclear bombs could have destroyed everything. Let that sink in.

Our plane took off from Idlewild Airport and a country snorting a bed of ashes held by millions of blood-soaked hands and landed in a sea of bright leaves and sunshine and brownskin men and women, girls and boys, looking like Adam and Eve's perky offspring. We flew from the land that rained genocidal fire on Japan to a country that exuded the gentleness of the cradle of life, with Oscar Niemeyer architecting the future in real time. The Kingston Hotel was a sumptuous fusion of Brazilian and Caribbean vibes and stood right off Praça da Liberdade. The lobby had vertiginous high ceilings and featured an elegant riot of teak and leaves, Francisco Goya's large sexy painting *The Parasol* setting a saucy romantic tone.

We were given our room keys and thirty minutes to

freshen up for lunch. My room was steamy. I didn't want to shower. I wanted to call home to Haiti and tell my father where I was, What an adventure! And I wanted him to tell my brother, my mom, everyone. Your son went to New York City to study and, through other talents and luck, was spending the summer in Brazil to try to keep the Americans from getting embarrassed in the World Cup! What an amazing kid I was, right? But I didn't call home. I couldn't. This trip, my football life's apotheosis, had to remain secret. My father wouldn't approve. I violated my promise to keep my nose in the books and not play football. My wife would freak out. Football? Brazil? What the hell, Gilbert?! You're supposed to be studying and now you're in Brazil playing games?!!! Just what you dreamed, right? More women to abandon me for? Fuck you! You better come back home, you black bastard! You can't run away from me forever! she'd scream.

No bueno.

Lunch was served in a dining room with glittering chandeliers lit up with a liquid glow reminiscent of stars. The shades were drawn. The food was untouched. It looked good. But when you pluck a dozen twenty-year-old boys from the muddy concrete jungles of Manhattan, Los Angeles, and Atlanta and plant us in a city and country that seemed to be a natural wonderland of endless fields of play, we didn't care about food. Our testosterone levels reached Hiroshima levels and climbed higher. We were excited, to say the least, too excited to sit still, but we were trying. There had to be *un appel à l'ordre*. Protocol.

Ron Banks was flanked by his wife, Cristina, Jose Garcia, the governor of Minas, German Herrera, the mayor of Belo Horizonte, the Garden of Eden of a city we found ourselves in, the capital of the state of Minas Gerais, and our bosses, Léa

Killdare, our handler, Charles Busutil, our head coach, and Selwyn Hinds, the brilliant and smooth coach from British Guyana who did the actual coaching and tactical work, especially for the match against England, only a week away. A former player in the Commonwealth, he knew the Brits well.

I don't understand why I remember Brazil in such detail during these last breaths of my life. I'm searching for my final words before I'm shot to death. But I've arrived at a period in my life story where I didn't have much to say. My mouth was often agape. I was in constant motion. I wasn't expected to say much anyway. I was expected to be a good teammate and performer, a living weapon for American patriotism and the war that football was becoming. I didn't have skin in the game, like I had in Haiti, a bloody history that scarred my black parent and stalked my white parent. I didn't expect much from America back then, and it gave me everything. Why isn't America stopping the dictator from killing me today? I'm practically dead already, but, come to think of it, the bullets and guns that will kill me are U.S.-made, like my fame. What goes around comes around?

Green is the color of life, and my memories of Brazil are awash in it. What else should I yearn for as the blackness of death envelops me this deadly sunny afternoon? I was nervous in that plush dining hall that night. Training camp in Florida a month before had assured me I was still a damn good player and could play well against anyone. I deserved my spot on the team. Except for one niggling fact: I wasn't American. I was a member of the American men's national football team for the football World Cup, but I was not even American, no passport, just a student visa that granted no professional or civic rights.

Don't worry about that, Dr. Killdare said over dinner the

night we met. It's a small technicality. It'll get taken care of before you tie your shoes to play in Belo.

We were in the 21 Club in Manhattan. Wood-paneled walls and gold polishings were everywhere. The only other black men I saw were the doorman and waiters wearing white gloves, and judging from the shock in those black men's faces, a black man as a dinner guest was as usual a sight as a flying saucer. Over steaks and wine and candlelight and cigar smoke, Dr. Killdare recruited me for the U.S. team with velvet smoothness. His team and America's team were interchangeable, like they were one and the same. This country that rebelled against the king of Britain had no shortage of patriarchs. Killdare spoke with the assurance of a man who had a habit of persuading the devil himself to sell him his soul. He reminded me of my father. He sensed my hesitation. He looked at his daughter. I looked at his daughter.

Léa here will make sure you're taken good care of every step of the way.

His daughter nodded solemnly.

So, are you in? America needs you, son. We really want to beat England. It's crazy, I know. Like landing a plane on the moon. Everyone is saying the English are going to wipe the floor with us. They're probably right. But you never know. We think you and your friends could help us surprise them. It's a new world, 1950. We shocked the world by dropping those nuclear bombs on Japan. The Russians thought they had us beat in the nuclear arms race! We want to keep surprising the world. We're special that way. We're good. You're that good. Léa tells me you're an ambitious young man. Straight A's, churchgoing. Think about the business we'll send down to Haiti if you help us out this summer. Play on our team. Lead us to the World Cup.

The scene, like the rich white man's speech, felt like the melody of a song Miles could have played, perhaps on his album *Ascenseur pour l'échafaud.* He played straight on that one, not sweet, but not quite sad, his customary melancholy was hidden, like in a game of hide-and-seek, or chess, a curious choice, considering the title and theme of the movie and album was an elevator to an execution. Menace was the order of the day. Miles let ominous bass lines and quietly sizzling cymbals do the work of creating a sinister mood with a light ebb and flow, leaving the listener off balance yet expectant, pleasantly, while wondering who was leading who, where were we going? To the gallows or to good times?

After accepting the offer I couldn't refuse, I grew obsessed with beating the English. In Belo Horizonte, we practiced twice a day in the week leading up to the big game. A morning practice ended around 9 a.m., right as the sun began to sizzle, and then we practiced late in the afternoons. The afternoon practice was my favorite, something about running on the best grass I'd ever seen in the late afternoon gave me extra pep, like when I was a kid in Haiti. The grass was fast and dewy, and looking up and around for the ball and seeing it fly in the sky framed by giant mountains, you could almost hear the birds and other animals stop their singing and playing to watch us practice, watch me prey on balls and defenders and smashing that ball into the net, over and over again, ignoring challenges and defenders and the keeper, seeing through them! Like an ogre in cleats. A football demon.

In the balmy Belo Horizonte evenings that week, I got to know my teammates in the most laid-back ways. We were too young to feel tired after two practices in one day, or perhaps we were tired, but we were too excited to be in Brazil as newly minted international football players to go to bed after dinner, dessert, and a cognac. I rather enjoyed capping the night with some rum and stories on the hotel veranda. If I stayed out there late enough, with my fellow homebody teammates, usually the Americans who had never been to another country before other than those where they had to kill people, a coach or two, and Banks, our cheerful host with the magical ability to conjure up an endless flow of caipirinhas, the players who had gone out on the town brought back good stories. Dave Harding was a good example. The very tall and handsome Air Force vet and central defender had been named the team captain at the end of training camp. In an attempt to cultivate his artistic side, he went out alone to visit São Francisco de Assis, the elegant church that was one of the Brazilian architect Oscar Niemeyer's early works. Playfully undulating along the Pampulha lagoon not far from the Independência stadium, the church's blue and white ceramic tiles featured stories of a priest in various states of exaltation. Dave was American, but the kind of stout, friendly guy who seemed like he could handle most situations anywhere. The head coach assumed he was a player who couldn't embarrass the team on the field and in public and would lead us by example. An easy assignment until he spent an afternoon sightseeing alone in Brazil. Near São Francisco, a pretty petite young woman came up to him and offered to take his picture in front of the famous church.

You're alone? She asked.

Si, he said, naïvely, thinking he was suave.

Her name was Ceu. She had big eyes and one of those big luscious manes of black hair that Native American women are famous for. After she took a few photos of Dave, she told him she and her friends were heading to the nearby zoo, and he should come with them. Yes, he said, again without hesitation. He had a wife and two kids waiting for him back home in Pennsylvania, but he gave them nary a thought. Despite his military background, he didn't think about the safety risks of getting in a car with a stranger his first day in a relatively poor country where he didn't speak the language. The American soccer federation didn't give us any security briefings or counseling on such perils. After what would forever be known as the Dave Harding Incident, Washington would correct that oversight. Dave piled into a car with four giggling women, yes, one sat on his lap, to go to the zoo. We wouldn't hear from Dave the rest of the week. *The rest of the week.*

At the zoo, the temperature climbed so high that Dave started to melt, and there was a band playing the infectious strains of samba. Everyone started dancing a little, a pep in their step as they gazed at orangutans and lions. Soon the music's bounciness grew so refreshing it drove everyone to distraction. They danced and danced in the alleys between the signifying monkeys and the kangaroos. The women touched Dave as they twirled their hips around him. They caressed his neck. They pawed his muscular body. They smiled sweetly at him. He smiled lustily, with a cheese-eating grin. He smiled and clapped and goose-stepped and sang *olé* on cue along with everyone in the zoo. Horns materialized and lifted the spontaneous carnival to dizzying high spirits. The congas and bells and whistles had the zoo feeling feisty, high. Giraffes bopped their heads. The horns, man, even the tuba, made Dave feel out-of-this-world happy. It was as if the disconcertingly light yet percussive music was carrying him on its shoulders like a conquering hero, a living god. He followed the band up and out of the zoo, the women clinging to him, their hips twirling at speeds faster than anything known to man, and certainly known to Dave. Ceu would periodically grin at him and kiss him on the cheek. She was so happy to have him with her, it seemed, and she didn't want him to ever leave, like she couldn't live without him, the most flattering feeling a woman could ever give a man, yes, the Brazilian women and the samba music made Dave feel essential, alive, more alive than his teammates or country did. The job that brought him to Brazil in the first place was forgotten. It seemed so trivial by comparison. Football in America didn't come with samba and twirling pretty women, did it? Football did, but not soccer. These new friends and these new rhythms and the cheerful clean air of this fragrant, intoxicating country had done things to him he didn't know could be done. He lost his mind, and he didn't miss it.

When Dave showed up in the hotel late that Tuesday night, two days before the England match, he reeked of sex and exhaustion. He could barely stay on his feet. I didn't know what satisfaction looked like until I saw the look on Dave's face that night. Coach was shocked but grateful he had returned. Like most of us, he also felt jealous. Who hadn't thought about disappearing into the wilds of Brazil since we arrived, football practice and big strategy meetings be damned? We were sick with worry, son, the coach said. We thought you were kidnapped! Or worse!

Kidnapped? Dave said, smiling dreamily at a memory. Nah. There were handcuffs, but they were all right.

Okay, I've heard enough. Selwyn, please get Dave cleaned up and ready for practice tomorrow.

Kiro Zelenikovski, our ace goalie, on the other hand, returned to the hotel one night with a more surprising story. For one, he returned with a beautiful eight-year-old boy in tow.

Meet my son, he said.

What? I said.

His name is Edson Arantes do Nascimento. His nickname is Pelé.

Pelé?

He's brilliant at football. Brilliant. Going to become a big star.

You know you can't keep him, right, Kiro?

He got sheepish.

Coach is going to kill you.

Kiro was fresh from Macedonia and wore his feelings on his sleeve at all times. Mercifully, on the veranda that night, Kiro was only with me and Banks. While he unspooled his story of newfound fatherhood, Banks positioned his seat for the best angle to see if danger in the form of a coach or indiscreet teammate was coming. Eventually, he took the boy by the hand and took him for a walk, leaving me alone with the latest teammate to lose his mind in Brazil.

After a long, snorting gulp from a drink, Kiro explained the cause of his instant fatherhood. She was a waitress in a restaurant in the Centro Mercato, he said. Even you would have fallen in love with her, Gil.

Really? I said.

I had developed a reputation as an ascetic or a playboy with impossibly high standards holding back his ammo. My teammates couldn't decide for sure which was true. Neither could I.

Yeah, man, she had the happiest eyes. I'm so used to pretty women with sad eyes. Balkan types. Hers were like stars! I had one meal, then I had a second meal. Then I started drinking. Juices, water, whatever. Then I drank a dozen beers to try to cool off my crush on her. It didn't work. Nothing worked. My appetite kept growing. She was sooooo friendly. I didn't want to leave. I just wanted to keep being seen by her.

Awwww, I said. That's sweet.

Her shift ended, Kiro continued. The market was switching to dinner mode. She went to the backroom to change out of her waitress uniform. You ever been to Praça do Papa?

No, not yet.

She had returned from the changing room, all dolled up. She looked stunning. Almost as tall as me! I never imagined someone could look so beautiful, Gil, Kiro said. She looked like Wonder Woman. I didn't understand most of the things she said, but I didn't care. I got the feeling, the gist, the warmth, the intimacy. I would follow her to Hades if she asked, so when she signaled with her head that I follow her, follow her I did, to her car. We eased into traffic, and I couldn't believe my luck. I was thrilled!

Kiro was a praying man, so he also prayed that she didn't kidnap him, like poor Dave, whose whereabouts were then unknown. The car was small and beat up and made unusual booming sounds. They drove through the city and then climbed and climbed up a hill, still in town, but high up a mountain.

I was getting dizzy, Kiro said, but I didn't care.

She stopped suddenly and clicked the handbrake.

Vamos, she said, unlocking her seat belt.

A beautiful piazza was laid out in front of their car. Its centerpiece was a giant cross that had an eerie similarity in size and hardiness to the one we imagine Jesus was crucified on. The spiritual charms of the cross and the scene seduced Kiro. He watched the waitress. She had been quiet for a while. They didn't understand each other's language and yet they understood each other. You know what I mean?

Yeah.

Her name was Helena. In non-waitress clothes, she was

youthful and leggy and smelled fresh like a waterfall. He watched her walk toward the giant cross with her arms wide open and head tilted up to the sky. Briefly the sunshine seemed to swallow her and the cross. Tears started to crawl down Kiro's cheeks. He followed her into the light. On the other side was a small band, a quartet, drums, congas, accordion, and trumpet, playing samba music. A crowd had gathered around the band, and they applauded and cheered someone too small for Kiro to see, so he got closer to see what the fuss was about. An eight-year-old boy was juggling a football with speed and skills that were otherworldly. Totally amazing. Kiro watched the boy perform trick after trick, juggling the ball with his feet and head and even his shoulders! He would juggle and dance with that ball running around the plaza. It was surreal! We were on top of a mountain with a little boy juggling a ball fantastically in the shadow of a giant crucifix to a samba beat and the pink fire of a setting sun. It was amazing.

I want you to have him, Helena said to Kiro. We were in her car with the boy, who turned out to be her son. She was driving me home, sometimes scarily. She had a persistent cough. It was bad, made holding the steering wheel a bit difficult and haphazard, scaring me. We snaked down the mountain and seemed on the verge of barreling off a cliff at any time to dive into the many bars of Belo Horizonte down below.

Word had gotten out around town that the American football team had settled in Belo for the World Cup, she said. She figured he was one of their players, tall and strapping as he was. The city was happy the Americans chose Belo, she said, and they were all rooting for them to beat England. England chose to base their World Cup camp in Rio de Janeiro, so fuck them.

Soon he ate ice cream with the beautiful sick waitress and her gifted boy in Praça da Liberdade, like a newly composed family. The sun set. The streetlights shimmered in the dark green forest. Fewer joggers, more families and couples killing time before going out to dinner. Kiro, Helena, and Pelé didn't speak the same languages, but their chemistry felt natural, easy. The boy was wonderful, and his mother told Kiro she was dying. And Kiro was in love with her, and he was eager to demonstrate his ardor was substantial and not fleeting.

Take him, she said. I don't have anything to give you in return. You don't really want this diseased body as much as you think you do. She opened a few buttons of her dress, and Kiro saw her unhealthy skinniness unleashed. She was a skeleton. Lots of bones that her skin seemed to be fleeing. Her begging was stronger than her body could take. She broke down into coughing fits. The coughs rang out across the entire central park. Birds flew out of their perches in panic. A woman was dying, angels sang. A young mother with one dying wish. That her son not end up an orphan on the streets like she had been as a child. That a good American spare him this dark fate. Kiro kissed the dying mother.

Okay, he said.

Obrigado, she said, softly, grateful, reaching out for her son.

Pelé ran to his mother and Kiro and hugged them both with his tiny arms, nestling his big head on Kiro's hip, his eyes closed. He didn't even cry when his mother waved goodbye and walked away, head hanging, long hair hiding her face, frail hands fumbling for her car keys. He felt in good hands with Kiro. The goalkeeper's big paws. His mother probably left him in the hands of strangers all his young life as she went to her various jobs, sometimes for days on end. She always returned to fetch him. He didn't know that night was the last time he would see his mother alive. Does anyone ever know that?

Kiro knew. His heart swelled with the feeling of honoring the last wish of a woman he loved.

Come on, he said to the boy, shaking his head. Sometimes love takes you in strange and strangely fulfilling directions.

I'm hungry. I live right there.

He pointed to the Kingston Hotel, grandly lit in the dark park.

That's your new home, Kiro said.

The boy nodded.

12

O NOSSO AMOR

Like many of my teammates, I eventually lost my mind to the intoxicating charms of Brazil too. I made the mistake of waiting until the night before the big game to leave the sanctuary of the hotel to check out the steamy nightlife of Belo Horizonte. The night was meant to be an innocent dipping of the toe in the saucy bars of a city known for its drinking scene instead of its beaches because, well, Belo had no beaches. It's an inland metropolis. Creating inward-looking tendencies, like binge drinking. Maybe the imposing mountains circling us started to feel oppressive after a week. When the night fell, the yearning for a watery escape naturally led to plunging into rum glasses. Maybe the pressure of being the one player expected to deliver goals for our motley crew against the best defenses in the world was getting to me. Maybe boxers don't have sex before a big fight, and football players should. Maybe my youthful arrogance made me think I could keep my professional composure when Brazil's heady cocktail of tropical weather, unusually friendly and sexy women and men, and omnipresent carnival music came for me. Like many generations of visitors before me, temptations won. They snuck up on me. The Haiti I grew up in was too neat, and my family was too respectable, so the louche corners were forbidden, even though they were hidden in plain sight. New York City's louche corners were obvious, but the city was too foreign, fast, and dangerous for me to explore the world beyond the college and jazz-scene bubbles. On top of that, the Big Apple was certainly too damn cold most of the time.

So, Belo Horizonte, the night before USA vs. England for the unofficial title of best Anglo-Saxon footballing country in the world, was hot and bothered. England claims ownership of football, the U.S. is an amateur trying to find footing in the Beautiful Game, as football is called. So why not a few shots of liquid courage for David on the eve of affronting Goliath? At Vicrobeck's, in the Santa Tereza district, I didn't feel like I drank an entire pitcher of caipirinha, but I did. Watching the owner-bartender, a smooth, very black man named Gilberto, ably move from tending bar to playing the piano and singing ballads that made women swoon, I felt like I was watching a very cool and sexy South American movie, while sitting in a scene in the movie. When the endorphins and liquor really kicked in, I began hallucinating visions of me corralling footballs and beating back English ogres to score goals. Black steel in the hour of chaos. Vicrobeck's easygoing multitasking gave the restaurant the feeling of being at your favorite uncle's house party. I began to relax in Belo for the first time. When the barman turned piano player belted Frank Sinatra's "My Way" with an unexpected yearning for power for his own salvation, the music crumpled my insides, and I began mewling. I bawled, man. I let out so many drunk tears that my pungent lamb shank went cold.

Let's get out of here, said Errol, a teammate. We can do better than this place, right?

I know just the place, Banks said.

Hamlet's was a strip club that sat in a sinister building next to a love hotel on a street packed with stray dogs. The moon was the color of a strawberry. The air still and pregnant. The boys and I did an impromptu pub crawl to get there. No one kept track of the number of drinks we had. The head coach was with us earlier in the evening, nominally to supervise and chaperone, especially me, the barely legal player on the team. But Coach Busutil never made it to the second bar and barely made it to the team lunch the next day. He made a new friend after a few stiff drinks. Everyone thought she was a man and not a woman, but she was a local delicacy of exquisitely ambiguous beauty. She whispered something in Coach's ear. He turned beet red and told us he was going to check out another spot down the street, and he'd be right back. The man-woman took Coach's hand and winked at us. What happens in Brazil stays in Brazil, right, fellas?

By the time we made it to the strip club, I had sampled so many drinks made with artisanal cachaça, the Brazilian liquor drawn from sugarcane, in so many bars manned by nice women with dimples and heaving bosoms, that I became an uncontrollably happy drunk in front of the parade of nude women at the club. They looked unusually pretty and sleek. At some point late in the night, I told Banks I was amazed how all the girls in the strip club told me they were only nineteen years old. Women that young couldn't work in clubs like this in America, I said. You might find one, but not a dozen teenage working girls in the same club.

That's because the legal age for prostitution in Brazil is sixteen, Banks said. OOOOOOOOOOOOOOOOOOOOOH!

I freaked out. We all did. We looked around the club with fresh, panicked eyes. All the naked women in the booths, at the bar, and on the stages were now, suddenly, jarringly, jailbait. If the legal age was sixteen, these women were all sixteen, if that. Strip club tradition encourages women to lie about their ages, add a few years, subtract a few, to stay legal, but never too legal, but damn, guys, this is wrong. Most of the guys left the club immediately, but I hesitated. If the girls were practically my age, did that count as breaking the law?

Then Reina Nubia, the star of the strip club, took the stage. Time stopped. Every strip club has a queen of the night. A thousand trumpets blared. Drums thundered. In Brazil that night she wore a glittering pink-and-yellow bikini, a flowing red cape, giant wings, a crown, and heels that made her so tall, her crown seemed to be grazing the ceiling. Our jaws dropped. When she finished her turn dancing on stage and came straight for me, even Banks was impressed. The Spanish football team players which had been sitting across the stage from us all night looked stunned. I recognized their captain, Marcos Losada, an imperial midfielder. The Spaniards let out a collective groan of disgust—him again?—and stomped out of the club. I leaned back into my booth and watched the queen of the night give me a private dance. I stared at the strobe lights sparkling in the ceiling. My eyes glazed with joy. I passed out.

When I came to, my head hurt bad. Why have the girls in this club been sending me free drinks all night, Banks?

The gentle Jamaican flagged a girl down and asked.

We're his fans! she answered. We thought he played really well today. All the girls want to go home with him.

But I didn't play a football match today.

But Chile played Colombia, Banks said. There was only one black guy on either team. And he had big hair like you.

My ego was deflated. They showed me love by accident!

They thought I was a star when I was a nobody. They mistook me for another black player! A star! And they were generous, and I took advantage. Like a loser.

It was two hours before the team breakfast, and ten hours before kickoff against England. Strands of white light from the dawning sun began filtering into the club, bringing reality and a reality check. It was time to go home. I was bummed out and suddenly very tired. I thought I was special. But I wasn't. Just another case of super-negro mistaken identity. Except I was an unproven negro. I was just another nigga with an afro. A young nobody. I wanted to go home. The tears came fast. I began to sob.

Let's go home, Banks said.

13

TWO–NIL

Cher Gilbert,

Good news!

I gave birth to our bouncing baby girl in the pastel green walls of the Maternity Center Isaie Jeanty this week. I named our newborn daughter Caroline Jill in your honor, the love of my life. I haven't heard from you in a few months, but your mom told me she told you about the pregnancy and how well it went. She became omnipresent in my life after she learned I was pregnant. She was even present at the delivery, standing in the delivery room, cradling the baby like the most precious thing in the world, gasping at the beauty of her first grandchild.

She really treats me like her daughter-in-law. You were right about how cold and efficient she could be. She seems to have blocked the Nazis' presence in Haiti out of her mind in much the same way she ignored Jackie your entire lives, despite living in the same compound. My mom was in the room when Jill was born too. Both ladies were hopping up and down, levitating with love. I was tired but happy to see them. Jill is amazing! A real blessing. Can't wait for you to meet her.

I hope this letter finds you and that it finds you in good health and spirits, my love.
Yours forever,
Aurélie

Aurélie put the letter in an envelope and put it away to be mailed after she left the hospital. When a shadow crossed Aurélie's face, her faux mother-in-law understood instinctively the reasons. She gave her granddaughter to her other grandparents and leaned down to Aurélie and whispered in her ear.

He'll be overjoyed when he gets this news, she said. He's been studying so hard the last three months to finish the school year with strong grades, even I haven't heard from him much.

In truth, Marie, Gil's mom, was worried sick by her son's silence as spring turned to summer. Even the spies she had her husband send to Harlem hadn't seen hide nor hair of Gil that spring. He was in good standing at Columbia University, that they knew. His grades were solid. He was a ghost, but a studious one.

The boy is learning a new world, her husband said, becoming a studious man in a hard country filled with distractions. It's not easy. But so far, so good. Don't worry your pretty little head about him. He's fine.

She repeated the advice to Aurélie, with less conviction. Aurélie didn't mind. She knew she was permanently linked to the man she loved even before she gave birth to their daughter. The love they shared was true. She could sense things were going well for him in New York City in recent months. She could feel his elation. Feel it rising too. In her bones. And her belly. The three of them, mother, father, and child, spoke to each other telepathically, across borders and time zones, continuously. Familial communion. Holy. The holiest, whether you had faith or not. The links were written in permanent ink. Their music fluted in its own frequency. The summer weather would do his spirits good. He did mention missing football the last time he wrote. She prayed the sport had returned to his life. Exercise would do him good, Aurélie thought. Really good, though he tended to lose his head a bit when the football adrenaline hit. His parents didn't know he was playing foot again. Aurélie encouraged his passion. It was their secret, a plank in their special bond. Football often turned people around her into childish fools, whether they played or merely cheered for players and teams. But Gil was brilliant at it. She wanted her man to shine, doing what he did best. Besides, with the pressure Gil was dealing with from his parents and school abroad, Aurélie hoped playing foot would give him some relief.

The next day, upon checking out of the hospital, Aurélie was led by her mother to a car full of women and girls from her family. Gil's mom was at the wheel.

Why is everyone here?

Hush, child, her mom said. Relax. It's time for a special ceremony in a very special place for you and your baby.

Saut d'Eau, here we come, added Marie Chevalier, Gil's mom.

The car peeled off and flew through the streets leading out of Port-au-Prince. Soon they were on the open road on their way to the center of the country and the town of Mirebalais. The open skies were azure blue and perfumed with clouds that looked like sweet cotton candy: fat, white, and light. They blanketed the sky like saints in the ceiling of the Sistine Chapel for as far as Aurélie's eyes could see. Maybe she was still high on medication from giving birth, or maybe it was a high from the sisterhood of this impromptu girls' trip with multiple generations of women in her family. Likely it was the dizzying reminder that there were two Haitis: One consisted of the Sturm und Drang of Port-au-Prince, a city that functions like a city-state, overpopulated, noisome, restless, and self-obsessed. The other Haiti was the countryside. *Le paysage* was peaceful, slow, friendly, and lush . . . Oh, it was lush! Aurélie and the girls felt richer grades of oxygen enter their lungs. When they ambled near the famous waterfalls of Saut d'Eau, they were pleasantly surprised by men who tipped their straw hats at them and women and girls dressed in white looking at them with the welcoming warmth of sisters. They could tell Aurélie was fresh out of the hospital. Saut d'Eau was a sacred waterfall for believers in Catholicism or voodoo. Millions of visitors came each year to bathe in the waters and pray for peace, health, and other blessings from God. The pilgrimage to these waters celebrated the Virgin Marie of Mont-Carmel, aka the Virgin of Miracles. The worshippers made Aurélie, a new mother, feel particularly welcome. However, the magnitude of motherhood now felt like a ton of bricks on her slender shoulders. She shuddered. Dear God, what did I get myself into?

Soon she was standing beneath the waterfall and feeling better under the cool rushing waters. They massaged her shoulders and slowly eased her anxieties. Yes, motherhood was a responsibility of epic proportions for many lifetimes, hers and her child's, but she was not alone. She was a child of God, and all mothers of faith are in sisterhood with Marie, *mère* de Jesus, the waters whispered to her. Aurélie gazed through the waters from inside a cave and watched her mother and Gil's mother gently dip their newborn granddaughter's head in the waters of Saut d'Eau. They then raised the baby to the sun with big smiles and brazen faith in a God of good things. They lowered the baby only after they felt for sure that God had acknowledged her and kneeled down from heaven to Haiti to pat Baby Jill's head and draw a cross on her forehead. Her grandmothers believed a good life awaited her child, and their optimism seeped into Aurélie too, like it had for pilgrim mothers in Haiti for hundreds of years. She didn't think about Gilbert. She felt empowered by the waters and her elders and their faith, and her faith, to do right by this child of hers. Aurélie stepped out of the waterfall, proud and in love with her child and motherhood. She waded into the waters and joined her mothers and child. Handed her daughter, she gave the day-old child her big brown nipple to suck milk from. Their bond was instant. Life begat life. Faith begat love. God is love. Everywhere.

On the drive back into Port-au-Prince after baptizing Baby Jill in Saut d'Eau, the ladies were greeted by an unprecedented happening. The flag of Haiti was everywhere. Seemingly all the houses and balconies were draped with the blue and red flag. When they entered Cité Soleil, all the kids held flags or draped them over their shoulders or wrapped them around their heads like bandanas. An outburst of national pride had taken over the city, but the cause of this euphoria was not carnival or politics related. We hadn't beaten the Americans again. It was the opposite.

It's Gilbert Chevalier, said an old man, staring at a radio and shaking his head in disbelief. He saved America!

The elder was sitting next to a radio broadcasting a football match when he saw their inquiring eyes. He didn't know who he was talking to, but he was eager to share the good news to people who seemed to have been living under a rock over the past twenty-four hours. His eyes were that of a man entranced.

Le petit Chevalier est fort, mes sœurs, he said. In Brazil, he scored the goal for the Americans to beat England in the World Cup! *We* beat England! We beat *England*! We did it!

Mme. Chevalier gasped.

Aurélie suppressed a rueful smile. The car slowly continued to her house.

One talented Haitian does something special for another country in another country, she thought, and it's a win for Haiti and all Haitians? *We* won? What did we win?

14

ORFEU NEGRO

On the best day of my life, I headed straight for the light at the end tunnel, holding little Pelé's hand. We each held a kid's hand as we walked to the football field from the locker room, a football tradition. On the field, I looked into the stands and saw thousands of faces that looked like mine. They cheered. My hangover dissipated. I felt their excitement was for me and me alone. We got this, I told them, with my chin up. The English players were big and blue-eyed, pasty and beefy. They held the hands of pale blond children. No mingling with brown kids for them. We took our places for the national anthems. I could see Léa, looking talismanic and cute, standing next to the U.S. ambassador, Wainwright Watkins, who managed to look both pompous and uncomfortable. I looked at my teammates, and they smiled or nodded back at me, like, we got this.

I was wrong. We were terrible. Starting from the national anthem, to which most of us didn't know the words to sing it. I hummed and tried to stay on beat, as the thunderous words blared in the stadium filled with uncomprehending Brazilians. The first words, those, I knew, then I laid out, latched on to the rhythm, clenched my jaw, then tried to look as imposing as people imagine a determined American should look. I sucked in my stomach and stuck out my chest and jaw. My wiry body stiffened. I can't remember the singer's name. I didn't dare break my serious pose to check her out. However, I did feel a thrill and chill down my spine when her aria climaxed with the line "land of the free." She held the word *free* for a beautifully long time. Her high pitch and stretching of the *eeee* was piercing to everyone who heard it that day. To my ears, she was singing of the joys of Haitian freedom too.

Of course, today, I'm in Haiti, a prisoner about to be executed, so the word *free*, and the subsequent words of the American national anthem, home of the brave, have special, twisted meaning. I feel neither free nor brave. My hands are tied behind my back. My eyes are blindfolded. My cigarette is unlit. I am forgotten by love and God, exhausted by self-pity and terror. I can't stop begging my executioners for mercy, nothing brave about begging. I'm going hoarse with it.

Ninety minutes into the football game against England in Belo Horizonte that steamy afternoon, I was mad too, but for prosaic reasons. I hadn't touched the ball! I hadn't touched the ball the entire match. Not once. A football game lasts only ninety minutes, and here we were, ninety minutes into the biggest match of my life, and I hadn't touched the fucking ball once. All my years of building skills and all my months of training and preparation for this day, I never received or snagged a ball to express my talents. To show the world what I could do.

All I did most of that afternoon was jog around one end of the pitch and watch my team get suffocated by the English on the other end. Their players were stronger and quicker than ours, so they pressed us high, as high as the keeper! Kiro struggled to get the ball to anyone, and our defenders could barely get the ball to a midfielder. Our midfielders were hogtied. They rarely got the ball, and when they did, they couldn't hang on to it. The English stole the ball from them like adults taking candy from children. The ball never made it out of our half of the field. We wore white uniforms. The English wore red. They seemed to see red whenever we dared to try to play football. They took the ball from kickoff and kicked it around themselves with ease, and they pelted our goal with shots when they got bored. Our keeper stopped every shot quite heroically all afternoon. The English kept inventing new ways to take shots at our goal. A goal or several goals seemed inevitable for England. The game felt like a practice session for them. They played like the greatest football players I'd ever seen. Poised, fast, sharp, decisive, strong, so strong. I'd run back on defense sometimes to help out my overwhelmed teammates. I just wanted to touch the ball a little, you know? But then I'd hear Coach Selwyn scream at me from the sidelines, what the fuck are you doing, Chevalier??! Get back to your fucking position!!

All week, morning, noon, and night, Coach Selwyn barked the strategy at us on the practice pitch, over breakfast, over lunch, and at dinner. In strip clubs! At bars, on the veranda. He told us the brutish English would seek to bully us, thinking we're weak novices, and dominate the time of possession of the ball, but that would be okay. We have a great goalkeeper, he'd say. We'll let them have the ball and tire themselves out. Even if they score once or twice, it'll be okay. We'll bend and we will not break.

This idea made my heart stop, but go on, Selwyn.

When they get tired, we'll counterattack! We'll get the ball out front to our freakishly fast and clever striker, and he'll bring us the win.

Oh, Selwyn, what did you get us into? The English aren't dominating us because we are letting them. They are beating the shit out of us because they're better than us! They're not letting us breathe. They not letting me touch the ball! It's like they have twenty players instead of eleven on the field. The only reason they not leading us by ten goals already is because we put ten men in the goal to stop all their fucking shots! It's illegal, but we have no choice. Their attack is relentless. Our helplessness is pitiful. I'm so useless!

And the English are not tiring. Nope, they are getting angrier, and their attacks were getting more intense. Oh wait, the English are getting a tad bit erratic too. The dejected crowd could sense the slight downshift in English precision. A smidgen of sloppiness from London. A collective groan has given way to a smattering of hope. Hope has a sound, you see. It's the sound of the sunrise. A light blinking on in a very dark room. Cobwebs swept away.

Wait, what's this? A clean relay of passes from Kiro to Dave, and from Dave to Errol, and Errol now looked to find me? Right before he gets mauled by two English players. No, three! A third player rams a shoulder into his back as two midfielders crush him, one taking out his legs with a slide tackle and the other with a kung-fu kick to the chest. Errol would spend the rest of the tournament in a wheelchair.

But he got the cross off! The ball was flying toward me! Oh shit! *Allez! Ça sent bon ça!* I could feel the English keeper coming for me from behind. It's me and you, big boy. Just me and you. Oh, you left your goal unprotected? You're out in the open field now, out of your element, in my territory?

Bad move, my dude. Really stupid move, in fact. Our research suggested the goalkeeper might be England's weakness. I had a lot of fun in the next thirty seconds. I controlled Errol's pass, still not even acknowledging the onrushing goalkeeper with his foaming mouth and murderous intent bearing down on me. But I felt elusive, light on my feet like a gazelle. I backheel the ball to my left, then I spin to my right. The goalkeeper misses me and grabs thin air and falls face-first in the grass. I gather the precious little black-and-white ball with my feet and kick it into the open goal. USA 1 England 0.

The referee whistles that the goal was good. He then whistles that the game is over.

I am the king of the world.

I should have run to my teammates' arms and shared the moment of our collective excellence together. But no, no, no, instead I ripped off my shirt and stared into the heavens and the roaring crowd in the stands and screamed my joy.

I am god!

I am god!

I did it!

I am god!!

PART III

ALL-AMERICANA

So I always struggled—especially early on—with the thought of: Well, do they not see the passion and fight and everything I put into it? Because when I would win it's like, "Oh, it's so easy." And when I would lose, it's like, "Wish he tried a bit more," almost.

—ROGER FEDERER, SWISS TENNIS CHAMPION

15

CORCOVADO

Funny how ten men can jump on top of your body as you lie in a field of grass in one crushing instant, and yet you feel no pain. In the bottom of the pile of overjoyed football players in Brazil that afternoon, I felt indescribably happy. My universe had gone black and smelly. And loud! My ears would ring for days from the screams and cheers of my teammates and thousands of Brazilians blaring their joy. I felt like God. Omni-everything. I did it. I fucking did it. My rallying cries lingered in the air, like radiation from an atom bomb explosion. When my buddies mobbed me in the middle of the field, it was as if they needed to touch me to make sure I was real, my last-second goal was real, and they, too, were real human beings living the most unbelievable moment of our lives, even after the referee's whistles signaled the goal was official, and the result was final, the game was over, our dream had come true. It lived! All their hard work and ridiculous optimism was well founded. Coach's strategy paid off. Selwyn was a genius. Victory materialized in flesh, space, and time, in something tangible, touchable, a man, a boy, with big hair, a lopsided grin, caramel skin, and a Jesus-like sense of miracle-making, discretion, brilliance, and timing. The Boy of the Veranda, some had started calling me when they thought I was out of earshot since we arrived in Brazil. I was the youngest player on the team, and I hung out on our hotel's veranda all the time. I was either too cool or scared to go prowl the streets with them, like they needed to every night. The moment I scored the game-winning goal against England, everything changed. My relationship with my teammates went from curious and casual to awed and grateful, What a goal! Thank you, thank you, thank you, they said. Ten, fifteen men screamed it, as I lay flat on my back with my arms spread in glory as if on a cross, and they held on to my body, eyes closed, cheeks to my skin and sneakers. They cherished the contact, and each person held on to the person closest to the person holding me to share an immense thrill by proximity. My greatness was now theirs, too, no matter our differences in ages, sizes, ethnicities, skills, and original nationalities. They thanked me in whispers. They thanked me in screams. Some of these men thanked me in silence, dry-eyed or tearfully. I felt their tears drench my skin. I heard their gratitude in a dozen languages and in sniffles and stares. I particularly felt their charged emotions in their touch, their grips, and their caresses. When they carefully removed themselves from their embrace of each other embracing, and, yes, crushing me, when they in turn picked me up in unison and put me on their shoulders and then their hands, lifting me toward their heavens, as an offering to God and gods alike, I saw the shadow of Hermes, the Greek god of games and athletes. He winked, as if to say, well done, my son from Germany–Haiti–New York City to Brazil, on this June 29, 1950. My teammates tossed me in the air to the chants of hip-hip hooray.

Hip-hip hooray! Hip-hip hooray!

They held me aloft on their shoulders, and they took a jog of honor around the stadium, showing me off like a new star and newborn deity to the Brazilians, who, in turn, now fully noticed for the first time that the football star born before their eyes in this unlikely victory by the Americans over heavily favored and very white England looked tanned, with big and soft curly hair and a fresh face with fleshy lips, much like most of their faces. The Americans recruited a Brazilian to beat the British Empire???!!! When Africans, from Morocco to South Africa, Rhodesia to Ethiopia, Senegal to Rwanda, saw black-and-white photos of me sitting on the shoulders of smiling white men like a hero, on the front pages of their newspapers in the next days, they assumed I was white at first. Just another picture of white men loving themselves, a common occurrence since the defeat of the Nazis. On closer inspection, however, Africans from all around the continent recognized me as one of their own. Something about my smile seemed familiar. Like it wasn't the praise from the white men that made me smile, but satisfaction with myself and the deployment of my talents. I was the star. Black Africans could mistake me for white at first but then they saw the hints of my quite lavish *métissage*, even in a black-and-white photo. They saw my One Drop. I was off-white. I was a soft black. Sepia. One of them. Arabs saw themselves, but sensed I was a little too polished to be Muslim, too carefree; I could be an Italian, or clearly one of those infuriatingly sunny people from South America and the Caribbean. Yet I was so comfortable, facing cameras while being held aloft like a child. I had to be Tunisian, right? Yeah, that's what I was. Or was I that cousin from Alexandria who rarely visited Cairo? In Asia, I was dismissed and admired as yet another

American sports prodigy. They respected my star qualities in that picture. The Europeans did too, but my excellence alarmed them. Calls rang out from chancellors and prime ministers' offices to their teams' coaches in Brazil participating in the World Cup. Orders given in no uncertain terms to coaches to ensure their players not fall prey to the arrogance and clumsiness of the English. The Americans are not to be taken lightly. They are meant to be crushed. They are lightweight, lucky idiots. They won their World Cup trophy by beating England in a relatively meaningless early match in the tournament. It's cute. But they must not be allowed to feel actual hope that their team is more than mere roadkill for serious footballing nations. If a head coach falls short of these orders, they might as well move to the Amazon jungle. Returning home to Europe would not be an option.

In the American locker room after the game, sweat turned to salt, ash enlaced necks, chests, legs, and faces. I sat on a stool in front of my locker flush with exhaustion that was starting to make me sleepy. I looked around at the ten men who made my scoring opportunity possible with great affection. Particularly the spine of the team who rose from suffering terrible harassment from the English attack to mustering the pass that facilitated the killing blow. One shot on goal the entire game, one goal. Victory. Football is crazy like that. My ego had grown to intergalactic dimensions, but I was no fool. A striker is nothing without his teammates. Every single one of them. I was merely the tip of the spear. Without the entire spear, I was a butter knife. Acknowledging my vulnerability to myself made me even more tired. I showered slowly, left the stadium, and clambered onto the team bus with heavy legs. I was oblivious to the crowd outside. People surrounded the team bus with a spontaneous carnival, the jarring Brazilian serenade. By the time the bus reached the hotel, the team shared my exhaustion. We were quiet, all deeply tired and sleepy. Suddenly, bleating horns jarred us awake. A massive carnival greeted us in front of the Kingston Hotel in the park in the center of Belo Horizonte. A throng covered every inch of the Circuito Cultural Praça da Liberdade. The lights of the hotel illuminated them like a beatific spotlight. Some of the dancing football fans rocked the bus gently. We walked out of the bus and, beyond the heroes' welcome cheers of all these strangers of all ages, I saw American flags draped on every window of the six-story hotel and the museums and other buildings around the plaza. I spotted the American flag wrapped around the bodies of the women and men and children dancing and playing samba music with frenzy and soul. Everyone in Belo Horizonte seemed to have become American overnight, thanks to me and my teammates shocking the world by beating England. The win meant a lot to a lot more people than I imagined. Up the steps at the hotel's entrance, I saw a safe, familiar face, so I ran up the stairs and lunged at her. She kissed me, hungrily, for the first time since we met months ago in Manhattan. She believed I was destined to become a great football player on the international stage more than I believed in myself, which is saying a lot. Kissing her that night, I was relieved she was right.

I'm so proud of you, she said, cupping my face.

This left me speechless. I needed to hear that! I needed to hear that from a woman in my life. It had been months since I connected with people back home in Haiti. I thought my life had become too surreal to share with my family. I was foolish to think so, but I'm learning that lesson the hard way now that I'm back in Haiti and about to die. An immigrant's life can be filled with surprises and dramatic twists and turns, but nothing compares with the speed and constant twists and turns of life in Haiti. Léa's juicy lips felt like the greatest fruit. I didn't see her wave off dozens of people clamoring for my attention as I kissed her and hugged her slender body for dear life, cupping her ass. She was always multitasking. I was a single-minded animal. I felt her hand cup the back of my head. The tenderness made me weak.

Take a bow, my king, Léa whispered in my ear, taking a necessary pause for us to catch our breaths.

I turned around to see what she was pointing to and gasped. The crowd staring at me and seemingly only me was massive and so colorful and excited in their red, white, blue, green, and yellow outfits and face paint. They were hundreds, maybe thousands of people, mostly Brazilians. Everyone was wearing the colors of the American and Brazilian flags. There were pale faces too, foreigners, clearly, European and American tourists and journalists and whatnot who had traveled all the way to Belo Horizonte, a city that, for all its charms and its location in the center of one of the most charming countries in the world, was resolutely not Rio de Janeiro, the most famous Brazilian city in the world, a hardy, sexy party town. Normally, Belo Horizonte was asleep by 10 p.m. Some foreigners came to see England finally beat the United States of America at something. But I was happy to disappoint them. I could see the wealthy young Americans out there too. I gave them a clenched-fist salute.

We did it!

Yeeeeeeaaaaaaaaaaaah, they cheered.

I was happy I'd disappointed the people who wanted England to beat America. And, apparently, so was Brazil and much of the world. The American team's multicultural diversity, and America's itself since Louis Armstrong was among the most famous Americans in the world in 1950, made it a much more attractive imperial overlord back then. As I die, I remember seeing people wearing U.S. Army grunt vests and helmets, shirtless with bikini bottoms, sandals, and army boots. There were children in strollers and folks in wheelchairs and prostitutes on a break from work. My teammates stood on the steps with me, staring in amazement at the crowd, some no doubt praying they hadn't come to lynch us. The crowd often bypassed them to look straight at me. I wasn't the only person wearing a USA Football World Cup sweatsuit who had given their all on the football pitch that afternoon, but they didn't care. They went silent when they saw me turn my attention from Léa. A hush of awe. *Merde!* What a wonderful feeling! I told her. What an incredible day.

We did it, Brazil! I shouted.

Isso!!!!!!!!!!!!!!! they cheered.

A riotous carnival broke out. The dancing was contagious, even my teammates tried a few samba steps. Horns were singing. Olés were being shouted on time. Hips were shaking and swiveling. I ran to my room with Léa, giggling with joy. We tried to make love, but I couldn't. I caught a cramp in my left leg from hamstring to groin. Freaked out—had she damaged the new American hero's golden legs, the one thing her father told her not to do?—Léa quickly dressed and ran down the hallway to get the team doctors. They diagnosed me with dehydration and prescribed me a lot of rest. Léa made a pouty face and reluctantly left me alone in my room. Coach Busutil looked relieved; color returned to his face. You get tomorrow off, he said.

Alone at last, I listened to the crowd outside the hotel sing my name in their foreign tongues. They serenaded me all through the night and cocooned my exhaustion. I slept like a baby with a smile on my face. Replaying my goal over and over and over in my head. All my grunting, heart-pounding, mocking glory. The happiest man in the world.

16

DREAMVILLE

Wake up, negro.

My eyes were closed. I was in bed, still tired, and now afraid to wake up, terrified that yesterday's victory in Brazil in the World Cup was merely a dream. After all, I had dreamed of it for months since I accepted the invitation to join the American team on their quest for the World Cup, even though I wasn't American. Haiti's historical imperial enemy is France, so it was easy to buy into the American David vs. European Goliath dream. Also, going up against the football giants of the Old World felt a little like reenacting my ancestral fight against France to free Haiti. I was too young and immature to have developed my own dreams of freedom.

Stop dreaming already, someone in my hotel room said. Damn. We're tired of waiting on you, nigga.

I heard the rustling of shades. Curtains opened, and the noon sun, hot and spicy, flooded my room. My sleepiness was gone.

I squinted one eye open. Nervously. Judging from the steaminess and the wild foliage in the park outside my window, yes,

I was still in Brazil, and not in Harlem, but did my team really play England and win?

It was Jackson, my teammate.

Rise and shine, pretty boy!

Jackson was going through my suitcase and picking out clothes for me. He was a huge Ugandan by way of Switzerland. Built like a superhero, he played football with great power and quickness, like a leopard. Even though he was in town for United Nations meetings, the recruiters got him to join the U.S. team for the World Cup after spotting him play foot with the gang on the Sheep Meadow.

Come on, Little Prince, he said, you're a king today, king of the world. Go get ready. I've been ordered to make sure you're entertained and rested today. I have a good group of friends waiting in a car downstairs to take us on a fun day trip.

I stared in the mirror in the hotel bathroom. Most of us spend our waking hours praying for dreams to come true. Few people have their dreams come true and see themselves in the mirror the morning after. The face I saw was my own, but different. Lighter, less burdened, blessed? Powerful yet fragile, skinnier. Do dreams make us look bloated, and accomplishments drain us of the extra kilos? I was still black, still brown, my nose was still bulbous. Lips fleshy. A shower. This brown body needs to smell better, quickly.

You're the toast of the planet today, Gil, Jackson said.

I could hear him through the bathroom door.

The Brazilians are calling you *Orfeu Negro*, Black Orpheus, a champion out of ancient myths. French newspapers call you the dazzling devil in cleats. The Americans are going nuts. They call you the hero of the new era of American football in the American century. The president of the United

States himself wants to talk to you. In fact, you have to call President Truman before we leave. The Chinese described you as a nuclear bomb dropped on England. The Indians were funny. They said you made the sun set on the British football empire before it even rose!

Ha!

In the hotel restaurant, I received a standing ovation from the kitchen staff and everyone eating at the hotel. I couldn't eat my croissant and orange juice in peace. It was humbling. The rest of the team had already scattered around Belo Horizonte. I ate quickly, and soon found myself in a car zooming down the highway toward Inhotim, a majestic open-air museum in the middle of a jungle. The two-hour ride on the BR-356 provided a great gulp of fresh air I didn't know I needed. I forgot to return President Truman's phone call. I should have checked in with Léa about my U.S. passport too. It hadn't arrived before the tournament started. If FIFA, global football's governing body, discovered a non-American played for America, and scored, the goal would be invalidated, and so would America's victory. It was illegal to have a noncitizen represent your country against other countries, who, presumably, fielded the best football players who held citizenship of their country. Unfair. A transgression. No one running the American team seemed to care about the risks of my illegal status and making it right. I should have cared. I would have gotten kicked out of the tournament and Brazil if the tournament officials found out. And having a U.S. passport probably had benefits I couldn't imagine at that age, at that time.

But that day, I felt extraordinarily good. Hermes from Haiti with an afro. Fresh, immune to pain, draped in glory. Danger-free. Forever. I didn't know that this feeling of self-actualization was extremely rare, sporadically occurring in a few lucky athletes' and artists' lives. I didn't know it would not last. I didn't know I would spend the rest of my life looking for that feeling again and never find it. There's nothing like the first tongue-kiss from God. There simply isn't. Most men and women live lives of quiet desperation, Thoreau said. He wasn't kidding. Nevertheless, that swell morning after my apotheosis on a football field, I felt the world was mine, and I would never ever feel blue. The magical jungle of Inhotim opened to me like a quirky paradise, a world of God-made nature and man-made creativity merged into one. Usha, a curator and artist, was our guide. I liked her. She was an unusually conscientious driver. When we got to the dicey rural roads of provincial Belo Horizonte, she calmly slalomed around chickens and dogs and naked children that wandered onto the streets. I didn't know the nature of her relationship with Jackson, but she made a point of touching him and smiling as if they shared a secret, and she was merely dutifully respectful to me. She told us there were seven hundred works of art by artists from forty countries scattered around this museum in a forest, some inside galleries, most embedded in the jungle, paintings and sculptures that were easy to spot, but she said it was equally important for us not to miss the exotic and beautiful animals and plants.

No touching the artwork or the wild animals, she said. They're both dangerous!

Hectares of grass without a ball to chase? I felt out of my element. My mind and body were wired for competition, physical exertion. Art and nature demanded my meek submission. The eclectic nature of this artistic patch of Brazil was forcing me to surrender my ego and switch open different parts of my brain. The colors, smells, and constant stream of creative visual surprises kept coming at every turn, everywhere I looked. Inhotim was determined to keep me off balance, with its charms. I'd read a lot of novels. *J'étais pas un abrutis quand même.* I liked music too. Music and fiction soothed the savage beast inside me. But these visual arts with their puns and political messages and gentle beauty were taking me somewhere else. A pointed dream state.

While we walked through the forest of Inhotim, Usha introduced us to a flower called the yellow ipê, a species of the Brazilian Cerrado. Giant yet light on their feet, thanks to their well-spread thin leaves, they were used in landscape design, notably in the making of barrels for aging cachaça, ah, cachaça, my favorite Brazilian drink. The silver-blue leaves of the Bismarck palm caught my eye too. There was something prehistoric about them. A half dozen stood between a lake and Hélio Oiticica's *Magic Square #5*, the most elegant art installation in the park. The nine brightly colored cement walls gave the impression of a gathering of buddies, or a football team's huddle of celebration. When you walked around the walls, you were inside a giant maze. Part hallucination, part . . . sanitarium?

I left those Magic Squares and joined my group of tourists, elated. They were inside one of the art galleries in the forest. I could see Jackson's big head in front, like a good student. Brightly lit like a doctor's office with paintings of various sizes hanging thoughtfully on its walls, the gallery in the jungle felt bracingly familiar. I felt like I'd walked into a gallery in the SoHo or Chelsea neighborhoods of New York City. Miles had dragged me to a gallery crawl one Friday night because he had his designs on a Swedish sculptor. What happened, Miles, I said, New York City ran out of white women for you, so now we gotta go up to the North Pole?

Miles didn't like the joke much, but it amused me then and also now. Inside the gallery, Usha, ever so pastoral in her transparent white-and-green robe and long curly hair pulled into a bun, whispered to show respect to the carefully curated intimate atmosphere. Silence was golden, she said, so we could hear what the artist was saying with his visual messages. If you listen to the silence, you may actually hear what the artist was thinking during each breath as she painted on a canvas or shaped an object during that particular time and place in their lives in their studios.

With that, she introduced an artist, Ricardo Ozier Lafontaine, youthful, bespectacled, and slightly stunned to be the center of attention and having to speak. We were gathered in front of a large painting of his, a subtle black pattern on a white canvas with a singular red dot drawn off-center. It was a *trompe-l'oeil*. I felt like the red dot moved the more I looked at it, slowly, changing locations, like the setting sun.

The red dot represents the heart, Lafontaine said. I'm fascinated by history, he added, particularly the history of black people in the world. Brazil was the last country to abolish slavery, in 1888. To put the date in perspective, Britain was the first to abolish this abhorrent business, in 1830. Brazil argued it needed more slaves, because it had a bigger country to build out. Some 15 percent of the population of the entire, continent-sized country. You could argue the country had more to lose because it needed the most slaves to drive its economy. I think history shows all the countries that made money off black slaves failed to pay them back by elevating them to partners in their postslavery economies. They missed out and still miss out on an opportunity to balance the moral scales. There's something edifying in doing right by a defeated man. We encourage it in sports. But we don't do it with black people in politics and business. We don't feel we owe them as much redress as we do, considering the wealth we built off the free labor of their ancestors. The profits we derive and continue to profit from denying them the conditions to compete with us fairly in education, the professions, industry, markets. We do ourselves a great disservice by shifting the responsibility to elevate their talents solely on them and not on us. We would be nothing without their labor. We are nothing without repaying our debts to them with partnership and justice. Until we do, we are an odd canvas with an off-center heart.

Lafontaine grinned.

A lightbulb went off in all our collective minds' eyes. Our befuddlement at his painting gave way to understanding and appreciation. His explanation of the vision behind the piece was searching and grand. *Osé!* What a metaphor! I had never thought much of the plight of Africans and their poor descendants in the postcolonial world. The visibly black are invariably the most downtrodden wherever they live, and it's not an accident, is it? Nothing bad that happens to black people is a coincidence, sheer bad luck, strictly the result of miscalculations on their parts and fate. We, the less black, thus closer to European, the European adjacent, the fucking people who had them work for us for free or a shitty share of the profits. We have to unfuck them. The shirking of that responsibility continues slavery, but it makes slaves of us all, addicts of an ancient hierarchy.

In the next room, a large colorful painting sat imposingly on an entire wall. A portrait of a *pulpeuse* woman in profile, she is staring longingly at a coconut tree and the ocean. The smaller trees and the jungle behind her are fading. To drive home the point, on closer look, the coconut tree surrounded by blue waves and sky is blinking. It's fluorescent, even. The artist wants us to see the woman's dream vacation, escape, or vision of paradise, whether the room is lit or dark.

I lost my mother at a young age, explained Christophe Mert, the artist, bearded, tall, and soulful. We remain in constant conversation.

Confronted with his longing, we, the audience, certainly me, the boy who hadn't called or written his mother in months, found myself thinking about my own mother and her dreams, for the first time. Of course, a part of my brain that I didn't visit often understood that mothers and fathers were people too, humans with flaws and charms. But dreams? What could be a better dream for a mother than mothering me? What dream did my father have besides bossing and coddling me? How could they possess other dreams? How dare they? My childish self-centeredness was stupid and quite staggering.

On the car ride back to centre-ville Belo Horizonte, I thought often about Christophe Mert's paintings and collages. He had a way of illustrating eyes, the dark vibrant eyes of black women, that stayed with me for a long time. Mert's eyes weren't haunted. They were alive. He celebrated the dreams of black women, and their meaning to him, with material cobbled from detritus and newspapers and magazines and signage in his neighborhood. It was as if he exhumed life from the garbage of the earth to celebrate the mothers of earth. Respect, Chris.

Penny for your thoughts, Gil?

It was Usha. Her eyes were on the darkening roads as she drove us along the yawning canyons out of rural Minas toward the big city. She was also watching me through the rearview mirror with intense curiosity. I could see why Jackson, a man who could have any woman in the world, preferred her.

I bet you Gil's thinking about how his battles against defenders and goalkeepers for goals could make for a good performing art piece, said Jackson.

Only if I die at the end.

What?

Remember that artist we saw who wouldn't explain her paintings?

Danielle Boisson?

Yes, her. We saw her paintings and asked her about them, and she said she didn't want to talk about them or sell them.

Yeah, that was weird.

I thought so too at first. Later I pressed her about it. I liked her answer.

What did she say, nigga?

She shrugged. She said her art is about the things all memorable art is about: life and death, heaven and hell.

Get the fuck out of here, Jackson said. She drew simple stick figures and palm trees and fire. My eight-year-old nephew in Kampala does that shit all the time.

Fire? Palm trees? Think about it, negro.

I smacked my forehead. I hope everyone doesn't think all football players are as rockheaded as my man Jackson. I might have to create art for real to distinguish myself from this lot.

After dinner in the relatively quiet hotel dining room, I skipped on going out. No bars or strip clubs. Not even a seat on the veranda to gossip and booze. There would be no victory laps with Brazilian women on my lap this night. No, no, I didn't order up oil and canvas to my room and start getting my Picasso on either. I sat in my hotel room with a pen and pad and stared at the park outside and listened to the quiet. I thought about Hemingway. It's 1950. What literate international adventurer didn't think about Hemingway and his stories about expats and surprising acts of valor and sacrifice, loss and grace?

I wrote a few letters that night, but I couldn't sleep.

Obrigado, Aurélie, mon amour,

A funny thing happened in the past few months. I got selected to join the American soccer team for the World Cup in Brazil. It's crazy, I know. I'm not American. I'd never played international football before so couldn't possibly be good enough. And I had promised Papa I would be a dutiful immigrant and study and only study while I lived in New York. I was supposed to resist the temptation to play football, even though both he and I didn't think there would be much football to play in America. Soccer maybe, but not football, the beautiful game.

Well, Mann tracht, un Gott lacht, say the Yiddish. Man plans, and God laughs. I certainly planned to be a robotic little migrant student during my four years of study in the Big Apple, but God had other plans for me. Football seduced me again. Like I had told you, I was just going to play regularly with some pals in Central Park, just to stay in shape. Just to have some fun, du plaisir sain. My nights listening to jazz, my newfound obsession, were wildly entertaining, but filled as those nights were with inspired music, cigarettes, drugs, and heartbreak, the dramatic kind, not the kiddie versions that happened on campus, they were anything but good for the soul.

Football, on the other hand, was soulful, pure, no one really won, nor lost, it's chess with the feet. Or something like that. I'm not much of a poet. I'm also tired. I'm writing to you from a hotel room in Belo Horizonte, Brazil. It's the day after the greatest football match of my life. I scored a goal in a World Cup game against England. We won! Team USA won. I guess I'm American now, right? I'm still working that out in my mind. If America is for winners, and winning is everything, I'm feeling pretty American today.

Chérie, I so wish you were there! You should have seen your boy! The move I made to liberate myself from the keeper and score in an open net was something I'd never tried before, not even for fun, while goofing around. It felt amazing! C'etait un coup de genie, j'avoue, immodestement.

On the other hand, I feel incredibly Haitian right now. I took a random opportunity to express my talents, gave the effort everything I had, and it worked out on the biggest stage. I was that good, and I didn't know it, but gave the game a shot, and wow, my talents were confirmed. You should see how happy my teammates and the Brazilians are. I gave my best to the world, and the world appreciated it. It's the most incredible experience, Aurélie. I feel so free right now. Free of my father. Free of every expectation anyone ever had of me. But please don't tell my parents. I want to keep this accomplishment to myself for a while longer. Keep it between us. You're my heart. Whatever I do when we're apart only has meaning because you exist. We're connected. You tether me to the best of me, this world. I love you so much, Aurélie Picard. The passion's so strong, it's embarrassing. My only life, my true happiness, is with you.

But we must be apart for a while longer, I'm sad to say. I might go play football in Europe after this tournament. Offers already started pouring in. For now, I feel satiated. I could easily come home now, but my show must go on. We have more games to play to try to qualify for the second round of this football tournament. I pray you're well. I can't receive any mail you sent me in New York City. By the time you receive this letter, I will probably have left the hotel with the name you see in the letterhead. But don't worry, I'll keep you posted on where this international adventure takes me.

Je t'embrasse fort, mon amour.

Ton homme,

Gilbert

Chére Mère,

Tout va bien a New York City. Il fait moins froid. Je travaille mieux. Je fais plus de sports a l'extérieure. Je me sent mieux dans ma peau. L'école va bien. J'ai fait des nouveaux amis, des immigrants, des outsiders, comme disent les américains. Mais j'ai des nouveaux amis américains aussi. Mon colloc est un musicien qui s'appelle Miles Davis. Il est noir-bleu comme un africain, mais très, très doué. Très connus. Même en France.

You should try to get one of his quintet's albums. I recommend "Birth of the Cool." It's an amazing, groundbreaking album. And also quite romantic. Jazz is my new crush. It's wicked, heady music. Give it a try, okay?

Et dit bonjour à Papa pour moi.

Je vous embrasse,

Gilbert

The dulcet strains of caressed guitar strings wafted up to my room with the evening breeze through my windows. I recognized the music of Jorge and Rogê, Brazil's finest duo. I overcame my lethargy, got up, dressed, and went downstairs. On the veranda of the Kingston, I found the entire football team enjoying a genteel two-man show deep in a night lit by a thousand candles. Someone had the bright idea of inviting the girls from the Hamlet strip club to hang out that evening. Our host Banks's handiwork, no doubt. A gift to celebrate your extraordinary performance against England, he said.

Every player and coach had a beautiful woman sitting on their lap, sipping champagne. Coach Busutil, a man of considerable appetites, had two. Nubia, the young queen of Hamlet's, saw me first and came and took my hand. She led me to the seat she had reserved for me. The song they were singing was "A Força." A force. I had become a fan of samba, a growing Brazilian sound, but the way the singer's voice broke when he sang the chorus made me swoon:

E vem do céu a força de Obatalá
E tem justiça na força de Xangô

Nubia whispered the translation in singsong in my ear.

And the strength of Obatalá comes from heaven
And there is justice in the strength of Xangô
And the strength of Iemanjá comes from the sea
And you come with the strength of our love

I couldn't let Nubia finish whispering the translation in my ear. Her voice was too sexy, the setting was too romantic. I was too tired, wired, emotional. I had spent the day observing art in a setting that left me overwhelmed by the natural world and the imagination. I was filled with unanswered and unanswerable questions about beauty, the meaning of my life and death, slaves, colonizers, sport, magic, and whether heaven or hell would greet me, and how they would feel, what they would make of me, what did God want of me. Did the devil help me score that goal? I had no answers. So many questions. Right this moment I held Nubia close to keep the singer's words from making me cry like a child in front of my friends.

I closed my eyes and let the song wash over me, feeling the clean, crisp air of all the Americas fill my lungs. Nubia whispered more lyrics to me.

And only love heals the pain
It's what makes living this day-to-day worth living
It has no end and it will always be like this
This love that only brings peace and so much joy
And only love is what heals the pain
It's what makes living this day-to-day worth living
It has no end and it will always be like this
This love that only brings peace, so much joy

17

SKETCHES OF SPAIN

Cher Père,

I hope you're well. I know it's been a while. A lot has happened since I left Haiti. It all happened too fast for me. Way too fast for me to share with you. I'm sorry I didn't find time to keep you up to date. I'm writing to you from Barcelona, Spain, by the way. Please note my new address. I was playing for Football Club Barcelona for a few years. I couldn't crack the starting lineup when everyone was healthy. I came off the bench and did okay. But then I got hurt. I reinjured my right knee. A flare-up of an injury from Brazil years ago.

I'm sure by now you heard I played for the United States' football team in the 1950 World Cup in Brazil. Crazy, right? It was an incredible experience, Papa. I know I wasn't supposed to play football when I studied at Columbia, but I couldn't resist. I played in Central Park, then I played for a local club. That's how the U.S. football federation found me. Brazil was amazing. I had improved playing with my left foot, as you always implored me to. I scored the game-winning goal against England in the opening game! We won 1–0. I was named

Man of the Match, but it was a team effort. Our goalkeeper played superhumanly. Our backline held off waves of English attacks. To this day, I don't know how they did it. We were so happy after that win! We forgot to prepare seriously for the second game. It was against Spain. They thrashed us 3–1. We scored early off a sloppy mistake by their defense. I was lingering, stole the ball, and passed to my man John Souza, with my left! And he scored. It was the 17th minute. We were overjoyed. We picked up where we left off against a strong European side. The crowd went wild. We were in a town called Curitiba. We expected a more hostile crowd than in Belo Horizonte, where we played England. Curitiba is in the wealthy southern part of Brazil. It's cold there. One of the colder cities of Brazil. Strangely, or not so coincidentally, the crowd there were descended from immigrants from Germany, Ukraine, Russia, Poland. To our surprise, they rooted for us! They booed the Spaniards hard. You never know which way the wind will blow with football fans, right? I suppose everyone likes an underdog, and we were looking like an underdog with teeth. We held our lead against them till the 81st minute. It was great. I was fighting hard to help protect our one-goal lead. I backtracked on defense a lot, Papa. Then I'd go on long runs to keep the Spanish defense honest. They attacked the shit out of us. They were taking shots from midfield that were actually dangerous. Eventually we cracked and broke open. They scored three consecutive goals. We felt dejected, like we'd lost 10–1. Like we didn't deserve to be in the tournament. I remembered what you often said about momentum, Papa. Momentum is for suckers. Real players generate momentum anytime they want. We have momentum each morning we wake up and get out of bed.

Well, the momentum of our bad second half against Spain

carried over to our next game, against Chile. It was in Recife, a large, funky port city in the northeast. They told us it was dangerous, and we weren't allowed to go carousing or nothing like that. The night before the game I felt sick. I had a fever. That game, we played like we all had fevers and were all blind and crippled too. Chile scored two goals before we could take off our warm-ups! We equalized on a dubious penalty early in the second half. Chile had an interesting striker, Atilio Cremaschi, that I learned a lot from. He was big and slow, but he was slick. He scored the last goal, the one that put us out of the tournament, on a bicycle kick! I tried to do those a lot. I can't even get one down during practice. But this fool nailed one in a World Cup game! We lost 5–2. Chile brought us crashing down to earth. We partied that night. Cried in our beers. The night wasn't all bad. I had a Brazilian girlfriend. Her name was Nubia. She traveled to all our games.

That relationship ended that night too. Some Spanish scouts liked the way I played during the tournament, especially against Spain, even though I didn't score. They offered me a large contract to play for Barcelona. And I accepted it. I figured you'd want me to ride the hot hand. Or my hot feet. Barcelona was a good team, but they were stuck in second place behind Real Madrid, the Spanish dictator's favorite team. They thought I could help them beat the long odds of dethroning Real like I did for the U.S. team in the World Cup. I couldn't bring my girlfriend along though, because I didn't have an American passport. The Spanish joked they couldn't bring two blacks to Spain at the same time. That would have doubled the number of black people in the country. And qualify as an invasion. They told me if I played well, they'd make me Spanish and then my girlfriend could join me.

They lied.

It's been eight years, and they still ain't given me the passport, Papa. Seems like I played well, but not well enough. The goalposts kept moving for them to keep rejecting the citizenship they promised. Seems like they didn't plan on giving me the Spanish passport no matter what happened, or how well I played. I did help Barcelona finally win the championship a couple of years ago. But then my bad knee started acting up bad. The team cut me a year ago. No other team signed me. I wasn't eligible for unemployment benefits. My agent—yes, I had an agent—he stopped returning my calls. I had to take on odd jobs to pay my rent. Keep a roof over my head. I can't get good jobs, despite speaking three languages and a year of accounting studies at Columbia University under my belt. Not having residency papers is blocking me from the good jobs.

Could you please send me a few bucks to get me through the month?

I'm sorry I had to hit you up for cash after being silent for so many years. I hope you forgive me. I had to try making my own mark on the world. I had to try to figure out if I could survive on my own without your benevolence. I know Haiti is better than living abroad. Certainly better for our family anyway. I miss you guys. Please don't tell Mom about my struggles, okay, Papa? I don't want her to worry about me more than she already does. Please tell her I'm doing fine. Just playing out the string on one last football contract before coming home. Most football-playing careers end around the age of thirty, so I'm not lying. I do feel like an idiot for letting not one, but two countries lure me into playing for them with false promises of citizenship. I don't know why I believed them when they kept telling me the passports were on their way. To be patient.

I'm never patient!

I don't know, Papa. I fucked up. I kept making bad deal after bad deal. I never read the fine print of the contracts. I never stood up for myself. My agent was assigned to me by the club to make sure I didn't cause trouble after they let me go. To make sure I go away quietly. I don't know how to make noise for myself even if I wanted to. I got used to not having my rights respected. I forgot what my human rights were. I seemed to have forgotten I was a human, with dignity. Me? Can you imagine? But that's immigrant life, it seems. One humiliation can lead to an avalanche, a terrible losing streak. Free falling.

I haven't stood like a man for a long time, Papa. I called on God, but He's sleeping. I know what you would say, God is always sleeping on Haitians. I let you down. I hope you can forgive me. And help, if you can.

Muchos abrazos,

Gilbert

18

PORT-AU-PRINCE ON LINE ONE

Mon Coeur,

I'm writing you to this address in Brazil because the letters I sent you to your apartment in New York started returning to me. What are you doing living in Brazil? The World Cup's been over for years. I'm at my wit's end worrying about you. Where are you, my son? Why haven't I heard from you? Not even Aurélie. Not your wife. Or your brother. We are worried sick.

While you've been gone, some good things have happened. Aurélie had a daughter! Her name is Caroline Jill. We call her Jill. She looks just like you. She was born with your great smile and eight years later she still has it. She's dying to meet her father. Tell me where you are, and I'll send you a plane ticket to come home. One way! Please. I know you're your own man now. We tried keeping up with your career. We're very proud of you. Especially your father. He's actually proud that you ignored his stupid ban on playing football in America and had a good World Cup for the Americans. We hope they paid you well for your hard work. His health is not so good, just so you know. All those years of chain-smoking cigarettes seem to have caught up with him. He doesn't seem to have that much time left on earth with us, Gilbert, to be honest. I'm praying for him. But he doesn't have the best karma. The business was doing well. It had stabilized. Then an awful new president came into power. A little man with a Napoleon complex, François Duvalier. You may have met the little demon in our house. He came to your wedding. He is raising taxes every week, and he has a gang of goons called the Tonton Macoutes coming around to harass businesses. He seems to be targeting your father. People are really upset with him. There's talk of revolution against this blue-black Napoleon. He used to be a doctor, you know. He wasn't even that good. Rumor was his practice was a front for him to seduce women for kinky sex. Your wife works for him. She stopped coming around to visit us after she lost her baby. Yes, she was pregnant. Don't worry. I doubt it was your child. After a few years, we thought she'd moved on to Paraguay or Grenada with her parents. Those Germans never fit in Haiti. But when Duvalier was elected president, there she was by his side. On TV! Can you believe it?

Anyway, write back! Please come back home. You've been away long enough. Harlem, the middle of nowhere Brazil. I'm sure you've had fun. I pray you have. I pray you're healthy and strong, my son. I can't wait to see you again! We both can't. Your father would be terribly happy to see you. Please hurry back. I'm healthy and strong as an ox, but my heart can't take missing you much longer. Port-au-Prince is hairy, but nothing you can't handle. Your country needs you, son. We all need you. Come on home.

Love,
Maman

19

HOMEGOING

I was depressed and sleeping that bottomless black sleep of the depressed in my tiny flat in Barcelona when the phone rang, and I learned Father died.

Oui? Non! I said. *D'accord. J'arrive.*

I can't explain exactly the reasons, but I felt then and there that my lost decade in Europe was finished. As if a switch lit me up like a robot, I got up, did a few push-ups, packed my toiletries and a few souvenir sweats, and threw on a black suit and tie. On my way out to the street for a taxi, I knocked on my landlord's door and gave her the keys to my apartment.

Au revoir, signora. Je retourne chez moi.

And the rent, *signor*?

I owed her several months' worth of rent. A humiliation from my inability to break through the non-football-playing job market in Spain or neighboring France. I gave her the card of the president of the Barcelona Football Club.

Call him for that, I said.

On the Avenida de Eixample, the sunlight had that faded gold shine that gave a romantic light to every moment of the day in this seaside city. The colorful Gaudí ceramics encircling

La Pedrera glittered like they always did in this light. On my bad days, their beauty, like the beauty of much of the Old World, fucked me up, like an insult, like they weren't for me. They couldn't be. They mocked me. Spain, like the glittering countries that bordered it, was a mirage for people like me, a constant reminder that I belonged in Spain merely as a tourist, the briefest visitor, not a citizen, migrant, or immigrant. Disposable talent *mais pas un directeur, un maître des lieux*. Never that. Proprietary interest was not allowed. Fuck them. I'm going home.

The cab fled the city. In a blink of an eye, we were in the countryside heading to the airport. I realized the city was small, like a borough in New York City, but struggling to fit into its bourgeoisie made it seem larger than life, otherworldly. The airport, this day, seemed trivial. With its big graffiti-painted wall, it felt infantile. Trying too hard to be clever, instead of utilitarian and solid, like Idlewild. Why did I take these people so seriously for so long? The passive-aggressive strain of my personality that had been dominant all my life seemed to have dissipated with my father's last breath.

On the airplane, I didn't make conversation with the man in the window seat next to me. He was clearly going to Miami on business. I was going home. Home. My turf. My slice of earth. Chauvinism tasted great. Mi casa. I enjoyed the best nap of a decade during that flight across the Atlantic. Back in Spain, I was reading *For Whom the Bell Tolls*. Now I'm like, why would a smart American fight in the Spanish Civil War when we had battles, or rifts to heal, in our own continent? Back in Barcelona, I lived furtively and sexlessly and went on long walks in old neighborhoods, avoiding tourists, police, and crowds, as was common for immigrants without legal rights, especially black men and women. Scroungers we were.

I didn't fear being discovered and deported. But I was embarrassed by my status and paralyzed by disbelief and self-pity.

Self-confidence and eye contact with strangers and hard-ons go hand in hand. Self-loathing ain't sexy.

The plane landing in Port-au-Prince didn't jolt me. I was too tired. I could have continued sleeping, but the people around me on that flight started clapping. Caribbean folks often clapped in appreciation of a successful *atterrissage*. Liberating homecoming jitters. I was tired, arms heavy. As if I swam to Haiti from Spain. The cabin door opened, and the heat of Haiti hit me full force. Whatever getting hit by flames from a blowtorch might feel like, the particularly heavy equatorial heat of Haiti is hotter. After quickly walking down the airplane steps, I didn't resist the urge to get on my knees and kiss the ground of my motherland. The humidity transformed my clothes into water. I walked in slow motion on the tarmac from the plane to the airport under the most blazing sun. Mouth open, heart agog. I. Was. Home! The Haitian passport that denied me so many opportunities to make a decent living abroad was greeted with bored approval by Toussaint Louverture airport officials. No side-eye from unwelcoming clerks. Being treated like a compatriot and fellow human, fraternally, shouldn't have felt so special, but I'd experienced its opposite brutally in Europe for a long time. The banality of communal acceptance felt wonderful. To the passport people in the douane, I could have been a long-lost cousin, uncle, or brother. I was family, for better or for worse, and treated warmly for that melanized fact. I had taken the affections of family for granted. I didn't understand why. I wanted to feel bigger than my family. Stronger. Invulnerable. Instead, I lived naked and afraid in a cold and abusive community with no familial relief for succor. Shame on me.

I walked through the airport renewing my vows with my country. I walked through the revolving doors, and outside the airport I felt like a man who had reentered his family home. The leafy mountains in the distance looked like wallpaper against the blue skies. The cars with their honking horns, the people crossing streets with that slow, unhurried Caribbean languor, the people selling souvenirs and snacks all along the streets, I noticed their faces, filled with sweat, worries, and familiarity. It was the very first time I looked at the faces of all Haitians from all walks of life around me, men and women, boys and girls, and saw myself. We had the same face, sweaty, twinkling, tough, alert.

My brother rolled up on me behind the wheel of a brown Cadillac. He honked the horn, pulled on the handbrake, and got out of the car. He wore his priest's white collar. Aurélie wasn't kidding. Jackie had become even more of a man of God while I wandered the world like a lost sheep. He hugged me.

Bienvenue, mon frère, he said.

I hadn't been touched in years. I hugged him. Hard. And I lost it.

Oh God, I'm so sorry, I said, bursting out in tears. I don't know. I don't know why I didn't call. Why I didn't just come back. I'm so sorry, Jackie. I missed you! I missed him. I . . . missed all of you so much. I . . . I . . . I'm so sorry!

He didn't say anything. He let me hold on to him and cry and babble my heart out until I was too tired to continue. He let me hold him for as long as I needed to. At some point, my legs went weak. I felt so much pain. I convulsed. All my years of confusion, of determination, of frustration, loneliness, furtive pleasure, excessive celebration, overcompensating, machismo, selfishness. Guilt! Missing Aurélie. Betraying her. Papa! Competing with Papa. Ignoring *Maman*. Papa. I didn't say goodbye. I didn't tell him I loved him. So much regret, so little excuses. So pathetic. So many living people to do right by. A dead father to honor. Honor? I lost track of its meaning. It's not a game. This much I was certain of. So much work ahead. At least, at last, I was in the right city and the country where I belonged. Home. The right papers. The birthright. Ancestral courage. An ear for justice. Faith glimmering. With my brother. Jackie held me up. Jackie held me up. Jackie held me up.

Slowly, he led me to the car door he had opened for me and sat me down. He took my bag and tossed it in the trunk. He started the car. Before driving us home, he took a long look at me. I stared straight ahead. Spent. My body was adapting to the strength that comes after the bone-deep exhaustion of pretending life is okay.

Your mother is holding up okay, he said. He'd been sick for a long time. I guess she had time to prepare for . . . to prepare. She's been running the business. She shouldn't be running the business.

I know.

Did those accounting studies stick?

Yes. Papa only had to send me money once, you know. I can handle things.

I pray you can. Your daughter is about nine years old.

My what?

Her name is Caroline. She's beautiful and smarter than you ever were.

How?

Aurélie. She's been single since you left too. Like she's been waiting for you. It's crazy, I know.

I have a daughter?

You have a daughter.

Oh my God.

She wrote you letters all the time, but we didn't have an address for you after you left New York. You don't deserve her.

I know.

I lowered my eyes. I lived like a savage rat in Europe when I had a family waiting for me at home here in Haiti. All that love was here while I was putting up with acres of bullshit in Europe. What an idiot I was.

Another thing: your wife is gone.

Word? Finally, some good news. She's not dead, is she?

No, Gil. She found a new man.

Oh.

Pretty soon after you left too.

Good for her. Anyone I know?

No. But you're meeting him after the funeral.

I'm what? Come on, Jackie.

Playtime's over, Gilbert.

Jesus Christ. Sorry. No offense.

You going to have to play nice with him.

Why? Why is he so special?

He's the company's and the country's worst enemy. He levies taxes against us almost daily.

What a dick. Sorry for the language. Wait, he has the power to impose taxes?? Who did Elizabeth hook up with? The president?

Yes.

No!

Yep.

The dictator?!

Oui.

The little ugly dude from Martinique? Power really is an aphrodisiac.

Can't be flippant with this one, Gilbert. Seriously. Tread lightly. It's personal.

I got no beef. I'll send him a gift in gratitude for taking her off my hands.

He doesn't know you have no beef. Not that it matters. Everything is personal with this guy. He has beef with people like you and families like ours. *He* thinks he won the lottery with Elizabeth, and, of course, he thinks you will want her back.

That's funny.

Not really. He's throwing you a parade. World Cup hero returns home. But it's a setup to size you up, put you in his pocket, eliminate you as a threat to his power.

How do you know all this, Jackie? Ain't you supposed to be too busy feeding the poor and curing the sick?

Father Jackie.

Right.

People come to confession every Wednesday, Gilbert. I listen.

Punaise, a parade. The last thing I needed.

Just remember the Ten Commandments, Gilbert. Especially the first one.

I am the Lord thy God. Thou shalt have no other Gods but me.

Exactly. That one.

The house in the hills of Pétionville looked smaller. The pink painting, chipped. The compound, shabbier. The palm trees, less leafy. Pale green, instead of *green*. Worn. Jackie's mom hadn't changed a wit or aged a day. Youthful, fresh-faced, healthy, athletic. She hugged me, her first time doing that. She took my bag from the trunk. Its weight stretched the biceps of her skinny arms.

There's hot water waiting for you in your bath, Mr. Chevalier. Dinner will be served at six.

That's a bit on the early side.

That's how Madame prefers.

Maman. Elle était dans le salon en train de donner des ordres contradictoires à un homme avec la tête d'un avocat. She looked like a woman who had been crying every day for the past decade.

Oh, you're here, she said, upon seeing me.

I got on my knees and hugged her as she sat on the sofa. I didn't want her to get up. She looked frail. I dared not acknowledge the amount of pain a decade of worrying about the whereabouts of her only son had caused her. Worry had aged her prematurely. At first she didn't hug me back, like she didn't want to allow herself the belief that I was actually present in our home, holding her, in flesh and blood and lapsed deodorant. *J'ai embrassé ma mère très longtemps en silence.*

Pardonne-moi, Maman.

Elle m'a pas répondu. I felt her tears snake down my cheeks. They were cold. Her skinny fingers dug into the skin of my back. She was shaking. Gathering strength. She cried without making a sound.

Let's go eat, I said.

I told the lawyer to come see me early in the morning. I held my mother for a very long time. I ate a very cold dinner, not alone, mercifully. Jackie ate with me, silently, mercifully. Mom went to bed to rest for the funeral.

The funeral was a dreary affair, enlivened only by the guitar strumming and maudlin singing of Manno Charlemagne. Manno possessed the closest thing to the voice of God Himself, deep, gravelly, rich, loving. He had the voice of every good Haitian father and grandfather and great-grandfather who ever lived and ever will live. His song "Lafanmi Vinn Peye San" warmed the wake.

The family paid in blood, he sang.

His song of my deceased father was incorrect. Papa lived a rich man's life and died of an indulgent man's bad habit, smoking, which he indulged in with no restraint like he indulged in all the pleasures of wealth, power, and good taste his entire life. I was the person who was going to pay for the protection of our family with blood.

The empty cemetery was a bad sign. The wake at the funeral home was packed with dozens of mourning colleagues, partners, friends, relatives, and policymakers and diplomats, and many, many other old sparring partners of my father. They were unfailingly kind, gentle, and worried. Very sad. Like my father's passing signaled the end of an era, bad times, and they would be joining him soon, if not literally then metaphorically. In my father's will, he scribbled a vague desire for a *tchaka* ceremony in his funeral. In old Haitian circles, death was a separation of the body from the soul, and the soul was like the wind, it came and went as it pleased, and never in the same form. So my German dad, on his deathbed made of Nazi-enhanced wealth, wanted to go out like an old Haitian wise man and receive a farewell that sent his soul to Guinea—Ginen, in creole—the African country we've come to dream of as our ancestral homeland. Keep dreaming, Papa.

He got a small send-off in a random corner of the sprawling national cemetery in centre-ville Port-au-Prince. It was just Mom, me, Jackie, his mom, our lawyer, and Monsignor Tilou presiding under an overcast sky. My mom came reluctantly. She came late. But she came. She needed help walking. It's like old age had hit her overnight, like a ton of bricks. She was joined at the hip to my father, after all. Her hips seemed as bad as his now, and he was dead.

My father was lowered into the ground, and the first patch of dirt tossed on his coffin. The shiny black coffin buried under black dirt was as black as he'd ever get. As if on cue, fog descended on us. Made it hard to see. The gravediggers had to pause. A throat cleared. The fog lifted, revealing a little bespectacled man flanked by a very striking blond woman. Giant armed guards stood behind them. Elizabeth and I made eye contact. I was genuinely happy to see her. We were happy to see each other. I went for a hug.

Don't, she whispered.

I heard a dozen guns get cocked toward me. I saw snipers in the distance too. Snipers. In Haiti. There were snipers in the cemetery at my father's funeral. What the hell?

I backed off. The little man looked up at me with softly evil eyes.

Very good, Mr. Chevalier. I'm sorry for your mother's loss this day. I'd hate for her to lose her only son too.

Everybody's tough when they have an army with them. Who are you?

Your president.

This is him? The infamous François Duvalier? The new

president of Haiti who took it upon himself to dismantle the nation's frail attempt at democracy and free-market capitalism? The asshole whose decision to persecute my father's business probably helped drive him to the grave? This is the pitch-black midget . . . who has been fucking my wife so well that she can't say hello to me in public anymore?

I watch him with mounting anger. He is smiling without smiling. Goading me with his sleepy yellow eyes.

Don't make me have to kill you today, son, he said. I'd like to. Don't get me wrong. My boys pack heat. They're ruthless murderers. Well trained. Look around this cemetery. I'm filling it up with disrespectful Haitians like you by the truckload every day. The gravediggers can barely keep up. But I need you. Tomorrow. I can't have a man more famous than me living in Haiti. Not for long. Not ever. But word has got out that you've returned. The World Cup football hero of 1950 is back. You can be useful. Serve your country, your new god. We're going to show you off a bit. I need to show the country that you're here on my behest. Let the people know that you ain't no different than all four million of them. You're my bitch.

Oh?

Yes, are you ready to be a nice little poodle tomorrow?

Sigh. I had one job to do. One measly job. Listen to my brother and not lose my cool in the face of this man's provocation. Be diplomatic. One fucking job. But I felt a violent urge well up inside me. Was it my vanity? Was it a call for justice? I felt I had to stand up for myself for the first time in a long time. To stand up for my family. To stand up for all Haitian families who suffered at the hands of this man's goons. So I blew the assignment.

That's enough bullshit from you, I said.

I slapped the shit out of the little bastard with the back

of my left hand. Cherry-red blood poured out of the wound my slap sliced open on his round cheek. He stumbled, head down. I looked at Elizabeth.

You could have done better, Liz. Evil never wins for long. You of all people should know that.

You're such a fool, Gil, she hissed. You're such a pitiful fool.

A commotion behind me. I feel the barrels of a dozen cold guns get pressed against my neck and head. We watched the little big man lift his head, straighten his tie, and pull out a white handkerchief from his suit's breast pocket and wipe the blood off his cheek. He looked at the bloody handkerchief and smiled that closed-mouth smile of his.

Mr. Chevalier, he said, looking deeply into my eyes. I believe the parade in your honor has been canceled. The rumor of your return to our beautiful Pearle des Antilles was just that: a rumor. A mirage. You got too bigheaded after your exploits in Brazil to return to being a humble Haitian citizen. You became too arrogant. You believed the hype. You forgot history. You became that most pathetic of creatures: a gringo. The public will be told you're still living in a castle in Switzerland, like a court jester, talking shit about Haiti and juggling balls for your supper. In reality, you're going to prison. Not just any prison. Fort Dimanche. My favorite place in Port-au-Prince. You're going to suffer. A lot. When you've had more than enough pain, I will double down on it. And then double down on that. When you think you're going to die from too much pain, I won't let you die. My men will know not to let you die. You will be broken, crippled, crazy. I'm going to hurt you so much you will beg for death. But I still won't kill you. I'll let you rest, heal, even dream of my mercy. Your freedom. Women. Then I'm going to drag you out of bed and execute you. In broad daylight. Death won't sneak up on you. Oh no, that would be too easy. Too sweet. Look at me, Mr. Chevalier. I am many things. I'm called many, many things. From Cap Haïtien to the *mornes* of Sainte Marie in Martinique. But sweet? Never sweet. I was born missing the sweet gene. I don't even have a sweet tooth. I was born without a kind bone in my body. That is my superpower. That is the reason I will live a very long life, and you will live a very short, painful one despite the difference in our starting stations in life. I come from the mud. You come from perfumed boudoirs. You never stood a chance against a man like me. People think money and kindness give men long lives. Money makes them soft and sloppy. Look at your father. Kindness coddles men. Dilutes the clever. Kind men didn't survive the Middle Passage. Clever men sold men into the Middle Passage. Men like me were forged in the Middle Passage. We got stronger with every kilometer on the ocean in the bowels of those ships, every whipping by the Europeans, every fumbled lynching. So many times, they left us hanging in the trees thinking we were dead, but we weren't. We were faking. Our strong necks broke ropes. Our hands broke chains. If you don't use enough of them, our heart can repel bullets. Kind men told the kings of Africa who sold us what they did was good. Just. Clever men told them the decision was shrewd and practical. An opportunity to rid Africa of their enemies, bad men like me. That God would forgive them. Right, Father?

Jackie was holding *Maman* and shaking. They both looked absolutely terrified. Why didn't they see this ambush coming? I did. In hindsight, it was obvious. No death is ever in vain. Especially in Haiti.

I don't do kindness, Gil. I don't need nor ask God to mollify my acts of evil. I don't hire speechwriters and playwrights and journalists to couch my evil in code words. I don't speak in tongues. I don't need no voodoo to water down the pleasure I derive in hurting men and women and families. You come for me, I hurt your family. That is my motto. Your mother knows that. And still she fomented rebels against me. Ain't that right, Marie?

You look surprised, Mr. Chevalier. Don't be. You mixed-race folks always assume you're untouchable. Above the fray. Your father may have lived his life getting high off young pussy. You may have lost your mind from the pleasures of celebrity from playing a child's game in foreign cities. But your mother, *elle est une vrai nègre. Pas une métisse. Une nègre.* She has more balls than any man. A model of rectitude and negritude, she believes in justice. She dreamed big and believes in the Haitian dream, the creation of a prosperous, disciplined, orderly country that sets the example and agenda for black people everywhere in the world. She believes in things like honoring the better angels in history and negotiating respectable terms with Washington and Paris and London and Beijing and Moscow for the improvement of all black lives and the world. Don't you, dear? To those ends, she was funneling a lot of your father's money into media, armed, and legal forces that wanted to check my powers. She has an army of lawyers on her payroll. Lawyers!

Duvalier laughed.

I got guns, bitch. I got infinitely more guns than you do. I got more guns than your lawyers have eyes, more guns than your journalists have pens and cameras. My guns are going to build this country, not no democracy. Not no voters. I got enough voters. I don't need more. The country doesn't need any more elections. The country needs you, though. The country needs you and your notions of justice and civility and equality to sit in a corner, passively. The people can have a glimpse of the Haitian dream. But they can't have the real thing. I will tease them with hope and then humble them with my reality. My forces are mightier than all pens. They will learn to fear and accept that. *Et oui, Madame Chevalier, tu n'auras pas de choix dans l'affaire.* Your presses and guerrilla forces will stand down. They will return to writing poems and tending farms. You will pay them to put down all weapons against me. Why? Because I will have your son in captivity. Your only son will be my Torture Toy. My innovations in torture will be tested on him for many years. He is strong. I heard ten men couldn't bring him down on a football field when he had the ball at his feet and the goal in his sights. He has a new goal. Taking the pain of isolation and imprisonment to keep you alive. To stay alive to keep you and the rest of his family alive. I will be hurting him every day until you die. After you die, which won't be soon, I hope, I will kill him. I know you know a good many Americans. I know a good many Americans too, bad ones.

You know the ones who want to build democratic and diplomatic fraternity and economic collaboration with Haiti. I know the Americans who want to win the Cold War against Russia. I can give them what they lost in Cuba. What do you have to give them? A hero? A martyr? I don't need no martyrs for a better Haiti, for so-called global Haitian excellence, running around. I don't need that idea inspiring boys and girls to chase greatness, justice, and fraternity for a better Haiti. Fuck them niggers. They don't deserve hope. I ain't letting you and your son give them much more than you have. *Non, Madame,* I ain't doing that.

On my whimsy, my men will eventually pump your son full of bullets. His limbs will separate from his body with their fury. All flesh will be ripped off his body by the ferocity of my bullets. Your face. That pretty face of his, which looks so much like yours, will be reduced to a skeleton by my bullets. Shredded. Completely shredded. I look forward to supervising their work personally that day. Goodbye, Mr. Chevalier. I'm glad I got to meet the famous football star, the conqueror of England. Gilbert the Great. This is the last time you will be seeing anyone who loved you alive.

With that, Duvalier caressed my cheek. Then he stepped back. In a hurry, his goons holstered their guns and lifted me off my feet and dragged me through the maze of alleyways in the cemetery, past gravestone after gravestone. They carried me so fast my feet barely touched the ground. The tombs were brightly painted and bedecked with flowers and framed pictures of handsome men and women. The artfulness of the flowers and colorful paint jobs of the tombs reminded me of the sentimental artwork scattered around the gardens of Inhotim. Haitians had a romantic relationship with death and the dead, and they carried on the romance after death, and presumably they met up and carried on those relationships with their beloved after their own deaths, partying in the afterlife, not missing the limits of their human forms. I can imagine them after they wake up in the pearly gates. I'm dead? Yes! *Koté, papi? En allé jouen frero. Bal la pral sauté! On va mettre le feu. Pour le reste de l'éternité.*

20

PRISON BREAK

The first few years in prison were not so bad. It's funny how much peace you might find when you accept your fate. The monotony, the library, and my living quarters were comfortable. No one asked anything of me. I felt no particular danger. I approached prison life like a monk in a monastery. My impulsiveness had caused my family enough trouble. A form of *sagesse* found me. Maybe Mom obeyed the dictator and stopped fomenting revolt against him. Maybe Duvalier forgot about killing me. The government seemed pretty busy rounding up key members of every important lightskin family in Haiti. These guys arrived by the busload every week. *La mulatraille*. The crème de la crème of Haitian society. Most were like me. Apolitical but noted businessmen, artists, and sportsmen. Low-hanging fruit, it seems. Culled to send a message, a cease-and-desist order of sorts, to politically motivated families. Duvalier, a man so darkskin they called him blue, as in blue-black, seemed to be executing a long-standing grudge against the lightskin elite. No doubt they made fun of him a lot as a kid. Or, worse, ignored him. Pitied him, too. But probably mostly ignored him. I'm guilty of it. Apparently he was at my wedding, and I didn't notice. Being short and darkskin in Port-au-Prince is a very tough beat, even for someone bright and driven enough to become a doctor.

One sweltering winter, living in a prison chockful of artists and entertainers delivered a howler. Jean-Claude Pelage, a poet and playwright and distant cousin, the running joke in Fort Dimanche was that all us mulattoes were cousins, we took to calling each other cousin, it was easier than trying to remember everyone's name, since mixed dudes do vaguely look alike, and there were only so many families with the power and soft hair texture, so yeah, what's up, cousin? How you feeling, cousin? And, more frequently, keep your head up, cousin, freedom might be round the corner, no point in committing suicide, cuz.

Anyway, Jean-Claude was among the prisoners on the unofficial suicide watch list I started keeping. The only words anyone ever heard him say during his first couple of years were: I can't believe this shit. He'd mumble them while getting food, the only times we'd see him. The rest of the time he spent in his cell crying or raging or sleeping.

I kept myself busy and entertained by coaching football and organizing tournaments. The inmates were getting younger and younger. Duvalier ran out of elders to arrest and started arresting their kids? I didn't understand. But the young Turks brought a lot of energy to the prison yard that needed canalizing.

I was standing in the middle of the football pitch, the exact spot where I'm about to die now, come to think of it. I whistled the start of a match. As I watch the young players chase after the ball like unleashed pit bulls, I saw Jean-Claude trudging toward me, something serious on his mind.

Cousin.

Cousin. Good to see you out of your cell.

Cut the crap, Gilbert. This ain't a social call. I don't know how you manage to be so cavalier about life in this hellhole prison. I don't get you. You had everything.

You can't imagine.

I can't! New York! Brazil! Spain!

Now here I am, seemingly cool with coaching football in Fort Dimanche while waiting for my execution.

It's fucking nuts, Gil.

How can I help you, cousin?

A play. *Dead Cat Bounce.* I've written a play inspired by the absurdity of it all.

Now you're getting the hang of prison life. Tell me more.

You know how the only way out of here is probably through an intervention by the American army, right? And you know how Americans easily believe the worst things about Haitians. Like, they seem to need to believe we turn people into zombies. We're cannibals. We worship the devil, et cetera. So. How about a play about Americans trapped in Haiti, and being forced to eat cats and dogs to survive? A group of Americans visiting Haiti as tourists. They get kidnapped and held for ransom. During captivity they learn how to eat people, cats, and dogs, and they learn the taste is not that bad.

You serious?

Yes! Let's do it big, a musical with songs about the wonders of eating real hot dogs!

Okay, calm down, J-C. You're not going to get the guys to sing.

Au contraire, mon frère, there are more good actors here than you think. We got Shakespearean talent here. And if we don't, I'll bring it out of them.

This might work. But before I greenlight this, how will

your play end? I've seen many plays with good premises that peter out by the end.

Hmmm, good question. Act One, Americans get kidnapped. Act Two, they learn to fit in to survive. Act Three, the Americans get word that their people are being turned into cannibals and cat-eaters in Haiti, they send the troops down to rescue them, but the new cannibals don't want to leave!

You're nuts, cousin.

A tiny bit.

And I love it! Go produce your play.

I watched Jean-Claude walk away. He had a pep in his step. Artists are like footballers. Whenever I go for a jog, and my heart starts pumping hard, I feel ready to score against anyone in any match anywhere, despite my creaky knees and worn-out reflexes. J-C's idea for a play about Haitians playing Americans who become Haitians and love it is nuts. But look at how happy it made him. I'm relieved to scratch him off the prison's suicide watch list.

21

THE AMERICAN

The day of Gil Chevalier's execution in Fort Dimanche, Aurélie Picard was uptown in Port-au-Prince, a down-on-her-luck lawyer in a rooftop bar in Pétionville sipping strong rum sours over lunch with a new acquaintance, a foreigner from whom she was hoping to raise money for her struggling nonprofit organization dedicated to defending the rights of humans with forgotten rights in sunnily cruel Haiti under a dictatorship. The man was a dashing and scholarly American named Steve Ritchey. His salt-and-pepper goatee gave him a pastoral vibe, but he was a banker, lean and fit, and his clothes, even his cream polo, looked tailored to within an inch of his physique. He radiated good health, fresh sunburns, and the excitement of being in a land of sweltering heat, good music, food, and dangerous people, the elixir of the Caribbean that has charmed visitors for centuries. Ritchey has been coming to the region for years, but wow, he couldn't believe he was in Haiti. *The* Haiti. Land of voodoo nights, sweaty days, menacing French creole, and heady sex, Ritchey has been to Cuba, Jamaica, even down in Trinidad and St. Lucia. But Haiti was such a black hole, no offense.

None taken.

It's massive, intense, and . . . French, with a creole vividness to the people that gave it an otherworldly vibe. Like Indonesia or the islands of Africa like Madagascar, he said. Or mythical, mysterious cities like Timbuktu in the Sahel. Haiti is the Timbuktu of the Americas, fascinating and creepy and legendary. And yet very American, the best of us, in a way, and certainly the blackest of us, if that makes sense.

It didn't, Aurélie thought. I hear you, she said.

It was such a random thing, this trip, he said. His church back home in Kansas began organizing the mission a whole year before. Everyone thought the idea of going to Haiti to be dangerous yet noble but as far off as heaven, so that when the day actually arrived to sign up for the trip and take a bus to the airport, they confronted the reality of Haiti, the black nation that had defeated Napoleon and recently scared away our bravest marines, and they decided they'd pass on the trip. Even Steve's wife passed on coming to Haiti, and he only converted to Catholicism for her. Their marriage had reached that point of sedentary bourgeois contentment aka sexlessness. The kids had graduated college and left the nest, on their own. Their own respective parents were dead and buried. Saying hello in the kitchen over breakfast and chatting about the weather took herculean effort. Sex was reserved for twice a year: his birthday and maybe Valentine's Day. On her birthday, she preferred to take a long walk.

Aurélie did not want to have sex with this man, so why was he talking so freely about his sex life? Then again she was also wondering if she was still attractive, if he found her attractive. She had put on weight in the past decade without Gilbert. She hadn't dated much. She settled into single motherhood and lawyering. The new president was eliminating and violating human rights in Haiti so fast she spent more time in courts lobbying to save those laws before they vanished than raising money to keep the lights on. Three of her colleagues had disappeared, fled to America or the Dominican Republic or just plain disappeared, probably swept into Fort Dimanche without a peep of due process, a disturbing new trend from the dictator's new government. She hadn't paid rent in months. Her mom was pissed. You need a man, she said. I need a grandson. Stop waiting for miracles. That miracle was her mother's code word for Gilbert. She preferred to think of him as Gilbert, the courteous boy who was unexpectedly and definitely the love of her life, and not Gil, the spoiled brat of the football pitch and high society. He left for college in New York City and disappeared in a haze of glamour and eccentricity and rumors. She *knew* her Gilbert would return to her arms. Just don't ask her when, or how. Aurélie had tried to stay in touch with him throughout the '50s. Their letters took months to reach each other. The letters affirmed their ardent love for each other and the boring routines of young adult life. Studies with deadlines that were easy to forget, fighting parents, lazy siblings, cars that didn't work (hers), asshole roommates (his), love of jazz (them both). When he succumbed to the temptation to play football again, she lost him. His letters became as infrequent as the lovemaking between Steve, the chatty American, and his wife. She thought the interruption would be brief. She prayed he was safe. She knew her faith in God's plan for them would get tested by the long distance at some point. That time arrived mercilessly. She still cried about it occasionally. When she saw couples that looked like them around Haiti. When she remembered how good and powerful their hug on the balcony of his house felt. The ownership she felt. The tenderness. The rightness of her assertion of her love during, face it, the worst place and at the worst time, the night of his wedding to another woman. Their familiarity and sudden intimacy could have been a passing event. Caribbean people are indeed very touchy-feely. This was their love language. But Aurélie Fabienne Picard and Gilbert Ernst Chevalier were deeply in love, and this love made the entire world its stage. It had no mercy for those who got burned by it. None whatever. Does the sun apologize for doling out suntans? Does fire extinguish itself? No, it singes. Everyone and everything who got too close. With no mercy. Everyone else was a bystander or collateral damage. Sorry, not sorry.

But in recent years, Gilbert felt gone. But he wasn't gone-gone. Where are you? When you share such a strong love, only death can take it away for real. They didn't run in the same circles, so there wasn't much news about him. Just rumors. There was a rumor that he had returned and lived up in Cap Haïtien with his wife, pumping out kids. She heard from others that he moved to Paris after becoming a big star at the 1950 World Cup and fell on hard times. This rumor felt legit, more than a *bri couri*, unverified news from the world off their island. It was reported by a dentist and neighbor of his family who thought he heard Gilbert's name during a France Inter radio broadcast, and that Gilbert was playing for Racing de Paris and playing well, then he got hurt. Aurélie didn't ask what happens to football players after they get hurt. Why didn't you come home to me, Gilbert? The hard times couldn't be true anyway since Gilbert was unusually lucky, and surely the Americans would take care of him after he did good by them in 1950. He had to be an American citizen now anyway. How else could he have played for the Americans in a World Cup? Haitians, sigh. We treat people who leave Haiti like deities or demons. They either leave to perform miracles on foreign shores to confirm Haitian greatness to a skeptical, hateful world, or they leave after bringing shame to their family via an unwanted pregnancy or political alliance never to be spoken of again. When thinking of Gilbert, Aurélie preferred to focus on the private joy of the love she shared with a beautiful and talented young man so smitten with her that he ruined his wedding to a skinny white woman for her in front of everybody. She was a thick girl from Cité Soleil, smart and devout with a great smile, but thick and from Cité Soleil nonetheless, and yet she had drawn the affections of a prince of Port-au-Prince *en flagrant délit*, as if it were the most natural, precious, and permanent thing in the world, like death and taxes.

Your country is wild, Aurélie, Steve said. People got stories! How do you know who to believe and who's lying when taking on the humanitarian legal cases you specialize in? Everyone's story is more dramatic than the last, and everyone here speaks with authority and charisma that makes them so damn persuasive. We don't know which charities to fund and which institutions care, or even exist, to help solve their problems with justice, health, security. Our driver compared Haiti to the Sahara. It's filled with mirages, and they're all convincing, but they're mostly ghost stories, nothing real. The craziest story I heard, Steve said, was about a prisoner currently on death row in Fort . . . Sunday?

Fort Dimanche, Aurélie said, suddenly snapped out of her reverie and paying attention to her interlocutor's mouth and every word as if they had become flames and the horror of horrors. Her truth sensor, and some other otherworldly sixth sense from deeper within, in the charcoal gravel pit of her soul where love lived, told her to pay attention to Steve's story.

Yeah, that place. There's word going around that there's a guy in that prison claiming to be an American hero, that he's in prison for nothing, and can't be allowed to die. Can you believe it? Apparently, he's been there for years. Telling everyone he can't be executed. Saying killing an American like him would violate international law, and the Americans would invade Haiti in retaliation and replace the president for ordering his execution. Can you believe that? Like we'd let one of ours rot in a prison in your stinking country. No offense.

None taken.

Aurélie believed him. Worse, she felt the pain and fear and impending death of this prisoner in her ribs and heart. It was real. It was overwhelming. He was doomed. But it can't be too late, can it? And, and, she sensed something else.

Are you okay? You look nauseous, Steve said.

I think the rum sours disagreed with me, Aurélie said. It's so hot, and I'm not much of a drinker. Does . . . does this imaginative prisoner have a name?

What's wrong? Steve said, looking alarmed. Water?

Yes, thank you, Aurélie said. I need water.

She noticed the sky above the rooftop bar of the Best Western Hotel for the first time. It was a pale blue and there were no clouds. Where were the clouds? She looked around for them, and the world spun around her faster and faster. Her chair disappeared, and the ground beneath her feet disappeared too. She found the clouds. They were dark and bunched up together and menacing in the distance, preparing to summarily hijack Port-au-Prince's eternal summer days with rain. Aurélie felt her spine stiffen. A storm was coming, and she had to brace herself. Her life was never going to be the same.

Phil, I think, Steve said. I think they said the name of this crazy prisoner in Fort Dimanche was Phil. Trust me, this can't be serious. Rumor has it that the prison is turning Americans into cannibals and dog eaters too.

Do you mean Gil?

No, no, it's Phil. I definitely heard Phil.

22

EXECUTION

Aurélie went straight home. On a table in the sunlit backyard, surrounded by plants, she saw her daughter doing homework. She applied herself seriously and mimicked her mother's body language when she was writing a brief and trying to figure out an argument or rehearsing remarks.

Bonjour, Maman! she said.

Aurélie hugged her wordlessly, like it could be the last time. Tears welled up in her eyes. She wiped them away quickly.

Let me look at you, she said. How's my hardworking girl doing today?

Great, Mommy, she said. I'm almost finished.

She gave her mother the can-I-get-back-to-my-homework nod.

I raised a dutiful little girl, Aurélie thought. It was a good life.

I have to go up to Pétionville, she told her mother in the kitchen on her way out. Her mom sensed something bad was afoot. Bad things often happened when Aurélie got mixed up with the rich folks.

Don't get home too late, she said. I cooked your favorite.

But her headstrong daughter's head was elsewhere. On another futile human rights case, she imagined. That girl buries more people than a funeral parlor.

Aurélie ambled her Peugeot into the Chevalier compound in Pétionville. She parked in front of the pink mansion and took out her backpack. She was surprised no one came out to greet her. Unusual. Times had changed for the worse for the country and clearly the Chevaliers were not immune. She opened the door and walked into the house. Father Jackie and Gil's mom were having tea in the sitting room. There were cobwebs in the corners of the ceiling and on the lampshades. Mme. Chevalier was stretched on a sofa with a compression towel on her forehead, like someone felled by migraines. Father Jackie was sipping tea with trembling hands like it was rum or moonshine and drinking a gallon of it hadn't been enough. These people were hurting. Wherever courage to go on with life came from, they needed it. Aurélie said hello like she was poking her head into an intimate chamber. Oh hey, they said with their weary eyes. She kissed each of them hello and pulled up a chair. Aurélie allowed silence to fill the room. They became family over the years. Aurélie worked tirelessly for Mme. Chevalier's nonprofit organization as the chief legal advocate for human rights. Father Jackie helped Aurélie out as best he could, mostly as the best uncle and last-minute babysitter in the world. This trio had also spent most of their time separately mourning the absence of Gilbert. They loved him dearly, passionately. They cheered and prayed for his successes abroad, but it was cheer mixed with fear and worry. The consequence of his footballing success meant his absence and silences, as he moved around the world for work.

His movements in these far-off cities and countries where he didn't even speak the local languages sometimes were made even more mysterious and nerve-racking since none of them had ever lived outside Haiti. They kept themselves busy helping the most troubled Haitians on the island. This was arduous work. Aurélie couldn't dwell on how the highs and lows of immigrant life were transforming Gil. Could he return to their small society and find a place? After the good times of life in North and South America and Europe, could Haiti be too difficult, could her company be too modest, could being responsible for others, such as his child and his father's crumbling empire, be too much for him to grasp? Aurélie could sometimes tell that his mom and brother knew Gilbert's whereabouts and a sense of how things were going, but they didn't tell her, and, out of pride, she didn't ask. They had to love him enough to give him the space he was taking by not keeping them updated on his wins and sorrows, and they signaled to Aurélie to do the same. She relied on prayer and faith in the will of God to protect her Ulysses in his wars on the football pitches of the world and balm her lonely heart.

She went on occasional dates, but they were disasters. She was distracted. She was taken. Once on a date that wasn't supposed to be a date after choir practice, a dashing writer with a square jaw and big smile was throwing her haymakers of game. The restaurant was the Fine Bouche in Bourdon, and the man had a silver tongue. He rained charming stories of his adventures and misadventures, and he also complimented her profusely and humorously. Grade-A romantic game. But she responded with wan smiles of weariness. Probably because of the residual effects of a humbling evening of singing songs of worship to the Lord, he got the message and relented. Some men can smell another man's grip on a woman's heart from a mile away. They're often too cowardly to fight it off and offer a more compelling romance. This writer, can't remember his name, Elias? Anyway, he gave up trying to seduce Aurélie and crawled into the coffin under the grave marked Friendzone by asking her if her boyfriend was on her mind. Acknowledging the boyfriend was the kiss of death. All beautiful women are being courted all the time, but le Boyfriend is a kind of awful cancer. The man who got under the skin successfully, too successfully, for too long a time and dropped the ball, rattling but not quite breaking the spell he had cast on her. His ghost is a pain in the ass no amount of denial can escape an astute gentleman, no matter how arrogantly he liked his chances.

We're on a break, Aurélie said, unconvincingly. *Je prend du recule, du temps pour moi-meme.*

Elias seemed to experience a sting. He looked like a little boy who'd lost a new toy. Aurélie *l'a mepriser.* She had no hope to give him. All the little bit of hope she held in her heart was for the mystery of Gil's locations around the world and cracking the wall of silence of his secretive family.

Gil's family had rewarded her patience by diligently treating her like Gilbert's long-suffering and loving wife and her daughter like their granddaughter and niece, especially after Elizabeth moved on. But they kept too many secrets.

Sitting in their living room, shrouded by tragedy, she went for hers.

I know about Gilbert, Aurélie said, breaking the glass of silence between her and Gil's mother and brother with a bluff.

Is he alive in Fort Dimanche?!!! Gil's mom said, bolting upright.

Her compress flew off her face and across the room. Aurélie had to duck to avoid it.

Yes, Aurélie said, keeping steady as her bluff proved scarily successful.

Father Jackie stared at his teacup like it owed him money.

He thought Aurélie was bluffing, but her answer seemed confident. She had his attention.

The Americans confirmed he was still alive and imprisoned in Fort Dimanche. But . . .

Gil's mother, normally impeccably composed, looked hysterical.

His execution is imminent. He doesn't have much time left.

Father Jackie broke his teacup. His hands bled. He cupped his head and bent down and moaned.

What do we do? What do we do?

I have a plan, Madame, Aurélie said, taking Marie Chevalier's hands into hers and working hard to quickly come up with a plan to save the love of her life from death in a gulag while pretending she wasn't shocked and happy to learn he was back in Haiti and only a few miles away from her.

We need to get the Americans to tell Duvalier to release him.

Damn right, they should.

Do you know the president of the United States? I know it's crazy, but after what Gilbert did for them in 1950, the least he could do is call Duvalier and order his release. He has the most leverage. I can't think of anyone else who could talk sense into our president.

Marie Chevalier sat back on the sofa and fell into a trance. She was thinking through the people in her Rolodex who could reach the ear of the new American president. What was his name? Kennedy. Pffit, he was young. She received a nice note from President Truman in 1950, thanking her for her son's service in the Brazil World Cup. What surprising class from the butcher of Japan. At the time, she thought it odd that the man who had just won an actual world war thought so highly of her son's performance kicking a football in shorts on grass in a tournament played in the middle of South America. But Aurélie was right. Men in Washington can decide the fates of boys like her darling son in the bowels of poor countries like Haiti on a whim. The world is unfair. Some people possess a lot of guns. But there's always someone who possesses more guns and bigger bombs to boss them around.

I know someone! Father Jackie said, startling the women. I know the U.S. ambassador. A fair-haired cat who lost his wife to tetanus last month.

He stood up, fixed his white collar, smoothed his black robe, and sprinted out the house.

The ladies looked at each other.

How?

Then they answered the question with the same word: Confession.

Gilbert's mother snapped back to reality too. Here's what we do next. Stop the fucking execution. We need to stall and buy time for Jackie to work his channels and get to Duvalier's ears. You have to go to the National Palace.

Me? Aurélie said.

She didn't like the idea one bit.

I know Americans too, she said, NGO leaders. I could go talk to them and maybe persuade them to bring medical help to Fort Dimanche and also ask them to put pressure on Papa Doc to call off his executioners. Release Gilbert.

Non, non, Gil's mother said.

She'd regained her rebel leader moxie. You must go to the National Palace immediately and cause a commotion. Create a distraction. I'll rally folks to Fort Dimanche.

Thirty minutes later, Aurélie found herself pulling her Peugeot up to the presidential palace, home of the butcher of Port-au-Prince. It was late afternoon. The sun looked nervous.

Light reflected off the windows in rays that blinded everyone. A young woman was entering the lion's den to persuade the woman whose husband she stole to resist exacting revenge and help save his life. Yes, Aurélie's life was absurd. She was on a suicide mission. Isn't that why love is called love? she could imagine Gil saying with that ridiculous smirk of his. The sun wanted the moon to take over. Aurélie's mission was too impossible to watch. The guards found her audacity curious.

Excuse me, miss, are you lost? A guard with black sunglasses said, poking her window with his machine gun.

No. I'm here to see Madame Chevalier. We have an appointment.

The soldier went to a booth to make a call. Soon, Aurélie saw the gates open, and her car was waved into the parking lot on the palace grounds by another guard. She walked into the building like she owned the place. The visit was her first. But her tax money was keeping the lights on, wasn't it?

You have some nerve, Elizabeth said, as a greeting.

She was standing behind a large mahogany table in a conference room with really high ceilings and an imposing chandelier. She wore a slinky black pantsuit and held a grudge the size of a minibus. They hadn't seen each other since her wedding night almost a decade ago.

Get over it, Elizabeth, Aurélie said. It's been ten years. We didn't mean to hurt you. You've done well for yourself since, haven't you?

The chandelier looked like it was made of dozens of diamonds. The wood-paneled walls and high-backed chairs made the room feel lavish and glamorous. The Haiti where Elizabeth lived was a lot nicer than Aurélie's.

Why are you here, Aurélie?

To exchange my life for his, Aurélie answered.

Elizabeth couldn't hide her shock at Aurélie's offer. Aurélie noticed she was wearing a glittering choker necklace around her long neck. She was into bondage sex. The rumors were true.

He's a big boy, Aurélie. He made his choices. *C'est la vie.*

We all make mistakes, Elizabeth. You're right. He has made a few more colorful ones than us.

Elizabeth almost smiled. Almost.

What's in it for us?

Us? Aurélie thought. No one voted you president of Haiti, Nazi. But she kept it to herself.

You send me to jail, and you remove the best human rights lawyer in Haiti from the board as you decimate Haitian humanity.

Not bad. But that can't be all you have to offer, is it?

You get your press conference and parade with Gilbert.

Go on.

The president gets to show off his sense of pop culture and people's touch in a photo op that will be watched by everyone who loves football, i.e., everyone in the world. Gil will make Duvalier look good, like he does for everyone.

And you can guarantee Gilbert will behave?

When he knows I've replaced him in his cell in Fort Dimanche, he'll do everything you say to honor my sacrifice. You know he will.

Elizabeth winced. She knew Aurélie was right.

You can go now, she said. We're done here.

Meanwhile, across town, inside the even more imposing conference room at the U.S. embassy in Tabarre, a priest is losing his mind watching twenty diplomats struggle to figure out how to write a cable asking their commander-in-chief to save his brother's life. Exasperated, Father Jackie took a deep breath, got up, and spread his arms, palms down, to get everyone to calm down and listen to him.

Guys, guys, guys, he said, excuse me but you seem to be wasting valuable time with this bit of admin.

Admin is our life, Father. We're diplomats.

I hear you. I hear you. But since you're sure the president will give the order to release Gilbert from unjust imprisonment, and time is of the essence, why don't we go get him out now, and have our respective presidents talk it out later?

Good idea! the ambassador said.

Isn't that dangerous?

Nah, Father Jackie said, you armed the soldiers guarding the prison, right? If we bring a small force and show your U.S. passports, they'll give you back your wrongly held citizen with no sweat. They'll even apologize for the oversight.

Yes, that makes sense.

The ambassador looked at his head of security. Why don't you round up a SWAT team and we head down to Fort Dimanche? I've been meaning to visit it for a report on its conditions for months. Two birds with one stone!

An hour later, Father Jackie found himself sitting on top of a tank rumbling down Grand Rue toward the infamous prison in La Saline. In front and behind his tank were two trucks filled with two dozen soldiers armed to the teeth. As they reached the port where Fort Dimanche sat to fend off invaders, the sea breeze refreshed Father Jackie's face. *Lui, le fils mal-aimé,* the bastard son, he allowed himself a smile for how his humble origins did not predict that he would become a modern-day apostle riding a chariot to lead a military force to stop a crucifixion in Haiti. He pushed aside the irony that the United States are the modern-day equivalent to the Roman Empire. What proved harder to dismiss was the disgust and fear that came when his convoy stopped in front of the wrought-iron gates of Fort Dimanche. It's a house of horrors that gave Father Jackie and his brother nightmares when they were kids, learning about the thousands of men and women who had been tortured, dismembered, castrated, starved, and killed there over the years and then had their dead bodies dumped like trash in a heap in the backyard. Also hard to dismiss for Father Jackie were the hundreds of dejected faces standing in front of the building holding signs demanding the prison's shutdown and human rights for Haitians. He recognized a few of them as protesters and political operatives employed by Gil's mother. Their long faces made his heart tighten. He walked through the sad faces and haunting silences with his armed battalion into the prison, touching his collar as if fingering a rosary for prayer. More sad faces lined the putrid hallways of Fort Dimanche. When he reached the courtyard, he saw a dozen executioners. The tips of their machine guns were smoking, as if the guns had freshly discharged their lethal ammo. Father Jackie noticed that the men had a pained look on their faces. They were looking at the ground, where Jackie saw Aurélie was cradling Gilbert's head. His long limbs looked loose and lifeless. His mother was looking at them and ugly crying.

Oh no, oh no, oh no! Gilbert! Jackie screamed. Are you okay?

Agonizingly slowly, his brother raised one of his arms straight up to the sky, and Gil showed his priestly brother a raised fist.

No one else moved or made a sound for a long time in the face of the miracle that had taken place in the yard that day.

Night fell.

Tree frogs began chirping their Caribbean night-song in the dimly lit prison courtyard. They sang a swan song for the day that was from all directions. Nature's surround sound. On the ground, staring into Aurélie's eyes, which were brown with echoes of the orange dusk, Gil marvels at the only face he'd been praying to see for so many years.

I'm dead, I surely must be dead, he thinks, and, thank God, I got into heaven, so I'm in my baby's arms, and the messy, scary, hard-to-love world on earth is below me, having played with me like a flag in a hurricane and destroyed me, but, but, but something is off, Gil thinks, Aurélie looks relieved and happy but also terrified. We need to get out of here. *Can* we get out of here? And I start freaking out too, oh yes, I do. I lift my head and look over Aurélie's shoulder, and I see a crowd of people in shock, and I see Jackie, a sight for sore eyes, but he, too, has a mouth agape in terror and amazement. What kind of heaven did you bring me to, God, if all my people are freaking out? Jackie was flanked by two people, President Duvalier to his right and my ex-wife on his left. Everyone was watching Aurélie and me. I became conscious of the fact that I was on the ground and kinda free. I tried to gather strength to get on my feet. I didn't know what the fuck was going on, but I'd been still long enough.

Father Jackie looked around nervously and became worried that the dictator and his consort were there to fight the deal to free Gil.

It's okay, Jackie, Elizabeth said. He's free to leave. We talked to the American president.

He can even stay in the country, if he wants, President Duvalier added. I love football.

Father Jackie ignored the words of Mr. and Mrs. Satan. A boat was waiting outside in the dark port to whisk Gilbert, Aurélie, and their daughter to another Caribbean island for safety. He had to get his brother out of here as swiftly as possible.

But he was too dumbfounded to move. Along with the prisoners, protesters, soldiers, family, and friends who had witnessed the miracle of Gilbert's rescue in Fort Dimanche, he was transfixed by the sight of his brother's raised fist in the twilight of the prison yard. The songs of tree frogs hiding in the bushes grew cacophonous. They, too, couldn't believe Gil was still alive.

What an incredibly lucky bastard.

Slowly, with the help of my beloved's arms, I clambered to my feet. I looked at my hands, and they were unchained. I touched my face and discovered that bullets hadn't perforated it. I opened my mouth and touched my teeth, and my teeth were there, even the purple one, no bullets had exploded them. What the fuck, God? I'm not in heaven??? I'm still alive. In Haiti. You answered my prayers and saved me? You actually saved me. I look at Aurélie and her pleading, happy face, and wow, I can't believe this. I can't believe this. I don't deserve this. I look up at the sky, which is ink-blue-black and as impassive and pregnant as ever. I feel the world spin around me at greater and greater speeds.

What the fuck, God?

And I pass out, falling into the arms of Aurélie, a soldier, and my brother. They catch me before I hit the ground.

EPILOGUE

Maman, how did you save Papa's life?

It's been six years since that night in Fort Dimanche. My family and I are picnicking under a giant coconut tree in Port-de-Paix on a white sand beach abutting a football pitch giddy with the symphony of children and adults at play. Port-de-Paix is a city in the far north of Haiti, on the peninsula west of Cap Haïtien. My father used to bring the family up here on vacation for respite from the barely contained anarchy in Port-au-Prince. After I got on my feet, I moved up here with Aurélie and our children. No, I didn't move to another Caribbean island or to South America for safety. Fuck that. God, I don't know why You keep blessing me with new chances at finding happiness. I really was ready to die. I still am very much ready to die. But since You insist on keeping me alive, I'm going to put my life to the service of others. I decided to keep living in Haiti so Duvalier knew I was keeping an eye on him and would sound the alarm globally if his bullshit got out of hand. Word spread of my presence in Port-de-Paix, and tourists from within and outside Haiti started coming through. Liberated prisoners of Fort Dimanche joined me up here *au fur et a mésure*. The town received new life. I picked up work in advertising and in coaching and teaching at a local high school. Aurélie was still fighting for human rights in the unfolding humanitarian disaster that was our country. There were still *a lot* of people unjustly imprisoned in Fort Dimanche that needed liberating. But on this late summer day, the sky over Haiti was an electric azure blue, there was grass, and it was impeccably green, the sand on the beach was fine like salt. The waves were choppy, but they were just showing off the white that contrasted so beautifully with the blue-green waters. The gentleness of this moment made me think of Miles Davis's tune "Blue in Green." He practiced that tune every night that winter after his breakup with Vero. It was incredibly sad. I'd eat my cold pizza with glassy eyes in my room, staring at the red lights of the cars trudging along Amsterdam Avenue, missing Aurélie, praying she wouldn't forsake our unholy but sturdy union. I didn't dare dream we would one day be reunited, create a family, and now be having a picnic in Haiti where Aurélie was trying to get me to eat a forkful of salad. Who likes salad? Not me. The way the fork hovered closer to my eyes than my mouth, the salad was feeling like a dual threat. Our five-year-old daughter, Nina, was transfixed by a football game, so focused she gave the impression that a hurricane and tsunami couldn't distract her.

You have to eat healthy, Gilbert, Aurélie said. I didn't save your life for you to waste it eating junk food.

That's when Jill, our forever daydreaming teenager, perked up and lifted her eyes from devouring Zora Neal Hurston's novel *Their Eyes Were Watching God*. She asked her mother how exactly she saved my life. Aurélie put down the fork, but I took her hand and guided it back up to my mouth and happily ate a mouthful of salad and grinned for my love's approval, sticking out my chest, miming a man with new muscles. A man-child in love. Aurélie smiled and looked tenderly at our inquisitive daughter.

You see, sweetheart, one time, when you were small, your father lost a fight with the dictator and was sentenced to death.

A fight over what?

Many things. Notions of love, family, patriotism, and most definitely freedom. The dictator thought freedom was optional for his compatriots and loved to take it away from us at the most ridiculous times. Your father rightly thought it was his birthright. He demanded freedom to grieve his father's death without being dictated to. That would be a cruel injustice, right?

Jill nodded.

And yet President Duvalier sent him to jail without due process and he lived in jail for a very long time. When I finally heard he was in prison, I told the president to take me instead and free him.

Mom! You did what? Jill said, eyes wide.

It was a gamble, I know. But I was hoping other people would rescue us both from prison eventually. My priority was to keep your father from getting executed. I knew the execution was coming, and, and . . . I didn't want him to die. The president agreed to take me into custody. What I remember from that moment was how casual taking lives was to him and his people. They didn't even bother to handcuff me when they took me to Fort Dimanche. There were a lot of protesters out front. *Tu vois, chérie, j'étais pas seule.* The fight for justice in our country is a movement. Not just me and your father. Your father was more of a celebrity than a fighter.

Yeah, Dad, how did you end up in prison? Weren't you just a football player?

This is Haiti, sweetheart, I said. We're all freedom fighters. Every day, and every single one of us. Even you and . . .

I looked at little Nina staring intently at the football match, oblivious to our conversation about the life and death of her parents and country.

. . . your sister. Given the misery and injustice around us, we cannot be indifferent. Believe me, I tried. But evil won't let you be blissfully ignorant. Or be blissful, period. Evil means hating another person's peace. Trust me on that one. Evil has a very long and relentless reach against black people and our peace. Worldwide too. So if we're not helping Africa regain dignity, we're hurting ourselves. If we're not helping our neighbors and brothers and sisters and strangers in need on these Caribbean islands or in the U.S., we're screwing ourselves. Anyway, let me shut up, Jill. Listen to your mother. My hero.

When I walked inside Fort Dimanche, the place was quiet, Aurélie said. I remember interviews I had with former prisoners of that awful place. They often spoke of the quiet that arrived minutes before an execution. The hush was oppressive and made them pray their turn would never come. I was walking in the corridor next to the courtyard. I looked in the yard and saw your father. Just as I casually lost my freedom and was ushered into that prison like it was a hotel, your father looked rather stylish in the courtyard that day. He wore a suit with a matching black blindfold, his feet were bare, and a cigarette dangled on his lips. His arms were tied behind his back. He looked tired. But he was screaming at a firing squad with guns cocked and ready to fire.

Jill gasped!

When I saw the soldiers take aim at my man, I lost it! I panicked, *chérie.*

Non! I screamed. I broke away from my guards and ran to your father in the courtyard. *Non, non, non!* I screamed at the firing squad, and then I stood in front of him and faced the soldiers and told them *non, arrêtez!* And the soldiers fired! But they aimed their bullets at the sun, the air. Mercifully, not us.

Thank God, I whispered.

Aurélie continued: They were disciplined, these soldiers. The protocol of executions meant you only killed the condemned man or woman and they were trained to stop at the slightest change in the environment. These killings were based on whims, after all. Maybe these men had killed so many people they were open to any excuse to stay an execution. Maybe, in their hearts, they didn't really want to execute Haiti's first football hero. And I gave them a good excuse to not do it.

What I didn't know, girls, Aurélie said, was that outside the prison, your uncle Jackie had convinced the U.S. embassy to tell their president about your father's predicament, and the U.S. president had called our dictator and told him he was a soccer fan and the dictator better not be hurting a hair on the head of Gilbert Chevalier, an American hero. Unknown to me, the dictator told President Kennedy that he wasn't aware of such a prisoner and lapse of judgment in his legal system and that he would go to Fort Dimanche personally to make sure your dad was safe. Kennedy didn't trust him and ordered his ambassador in Haiti to bring troops to Fort Dimanche to rescue your father. I didn't know all that. When the soldiers put their guns down, I turned around and took off your father's blindfold. He had been chattering jibberish. What's happening?! What's happening???!!!! Am I dead? Why don't I feel anything??

When he saw me, he looked hysterical and was so sweet.

Aurélie?! he said, it's you! *C'est vraiment toi. Tu m'as sauvé! Merci, chérie. Merci, Dieu. Merci! Merci! Mesi!!!*

Then he passed out in my arms, we fell to the ground together. The Americans made the dictator let both of us leave. We've been holding on to each other tightly ever since.

When Aurélie finished the story, she looked at me with eyes full of love. I looked calm but inside I recoiled with fear. I felt an acute pain in my heart's arteries like you wouldn't believe! I relived the fear I experienced the moment I thought I was killed. The terror and shock and awe. It's so awful, God. Yes, You, God, I'm addressing You. I'm still mad at You. I was in pain for so long! I was lost in the world, starving for affection, lunging at every shred of admiration, like an idiot, so desperate, so foolish, for so many years, too many, what was the point of making me so gifted only to reduce me to helplessness when faced with the whims of man? What was the point of so many highs, so much happiness, Brazil? When You or the devil's minions could snuff out my joys with a sigh, like a candle. I haven't been the same since Fort Dimanche. My ego died that day. *Non*, not that day, in the years of misery leading up to that. My faith in You, God, received a crippling blow. Since then, I move around the world afraid of my own shadow. Low confidence. No strength. Clinging to my wife's skirts for protection. What happens to a man who lived out great dreams then suffered at the hands of fools and ghouls? He ends up like me? Going through life wondering if God ever loved him. How could He if all God's blessings let me suffer so much at the hands of men gifted at inflicting nothing but pain and humiliation?

The Roman poet Ovid wrote, Love is a scam—every time, every case, in his book *The Art of Love*, Ars Amatoria. The book got him in trouble with the Roman emperor of the time. That emperor believed in the sanctity of love, especially family and marriage, and couldn't handle a poet's doubts. Fucking emperors and dictators and their certainties. I'm not a poet, but I'm all doubts, God. I'm giving You the side-eye every Sunday at church. Maybe Your love is a fucking scam. Is Your love the ultimate dick tease? Can I ever trust it? When can I relax when I know what feral hate can do? I've experienced the greatest love of all and the most sinister hate one can experience. I know I'm Haitian, and that is our lot, but even by the epic standards of melodramatic Haitian life, You fucked me up, God. You did me dirty. You gave me a great life, and You killed it and me, and yet You let me live. Whither joy? What is safe? What the fuck can I trust in this shifty, savage world of Yours? You killed Gil Chevalier, football star, and You left me with Gilbert Chevalier, family man. Am I worthy? Will I be good enough?

As if on cue, a football whistled past our faces across the picnic blanket toward the Atlantic Ocean. In a flash, Nina chased the ball down and nabbed it before the waters could. She dribbled the ball with her feet and knees and head from the edge of the sea to the football pitch, where she finished her juggling of the ball by grandly kicking it to the group of players. They cheered in gratitude. Come play with us, they asked Nina.

I was shocked. I gave her a football at birth, of course, and

I've seen her play around with her friends here and there over the years. But I had no idea our Nina had developed significant gifts, with speed and skills even I didn't have at her age.

She turned to us and said, Can I?

Yes, you can, Aurélie said. Have fun. We'll wait for you right here.

Go get them, sweetheart, I added.

I watched my daughter survey the field of play. It was filled with boys and girls, men and women, of all ages and colors chasing and kicking a ball on green grass on a spectacularly sunny afternoon. I smiled when she ran to play with them with all the speed her tiny legs could muster.

She lost herself in football, never once looking back at me, her mom, or her sister.

I'm not certain what God wants of me, and I definitely don't know what He will do to me and mine next. But today, there is football, and it is still a beautiful, mysterious, and simple game. I guess I'll keep enjoying that while I can.

ACKNOWLEDGMENTS

No man is an island, even a novelist living on a Caribbean island. So this long-gestating novel exists because of the loving support of a lot of people. The people of Martinique, first of all, notably my friends Sandrine Desire, Sarita Fanfant Smith, Dany and Edith Bruere-Dawson, Aurélie Armand, Nathaly Psyché, Gaelle Picard, Yann Desire, Céline Campi, Philippe-Alexandre Cayol, Helene Oreve, Sebastien Ali, Kathleen Maran, Patricia Conflon, Dominique Dérond, Rebekah Loche-Ertus, Valery Psyché, Caroline Ozier-Lafontaine, and Gilles Vicrobeck. You took me in like family a few years ago, and your passion for faith, literature, and the arts unlocked my writer's block. Mesi an chay!

Thank you to my far-flung yet steadfast friends: my sister Marie-Yves Léger, my cousins Michael "Sha Money XL" Clervoix and Pascal Duroseau, and my friends Dave Harding, Veronica Chambers, Edwidge Danticat, Steven Ritchey, Peter Druian, Danielle Boursiquot, Nick Chiles, Justin Fox, Musoke J. Sempala, Lauri Jalanti, Marten Gillgren, Marcos Losada, Daniel George, Junot Díaz, Rachelle Riley, Muriel Philibert, Joel Dreyfuss, German Herrera, Errol Cockfield,

Ken Kurson, Marc Boxser, Jan Klawitter, Kiro Zelenikovski, Carsten Snedker in Brazil, Ron Banks, Charles Moore, Charles Busutil, Lorentza Ruud, Sunita Palekar, Serge Stepanov, and Marvin Barksdale.

And a huge thank-you to the team that took this book off my laptop and transformed it into a physical dream come true: my agents at UTA, Christy Fletcher and Veronica Goldstein, and my editors at MCD and Farrar, Straus and Giroux, Benjamin Brooks and Sean McDonald.

A NOTE ABOUT THE AUTHOR

Dimitry Elias Léger is the author of *God Loves Haiti*, a finalist for the PEN Open Book Award. His writing has appeared in *The New York Times*, *Time*, *Fortune*, *Granta*, the *Miami Herald*, *Literary Hub*, *The Millions*, and *The Source*. Léger studied geopolitics at Harvard's Kennedy School of Government and served as an adviser to the United Nations for a decade. He divides his time between Brooklyn, Geneva, and Martinique.